^a Roommate ^{for} Christmas

Contents

To everyone who loves a cheesy Christmas movie.

Prologue

"Chicago sure is beautiful at Christmastime."

Startled, Paige Ellis turned to see Gerry from HR standing right behind her.

She had been lost in thought looking out toward the heart of downtown Chicago from the rooftop bar of LondonHouse, where her company was hosting their annual Christmas party. It was chilly and getting windy, but it was hard to pass up an opportunity to see this view.

"It sure is," she replied lazily. "Excuse me, time for a refill," she said as she looked down at her only half-empty glass of wine and then proceeded to chug it. The last thing she wanted was to get roped into looking at photos of Gerry's pet iguanas again.

Besides, Paige hadn't seen Chance since they arrived together an hour earlier, and she wanted to check up on him. She had been slightly miffed that he ditched her as soon as they walked in, probably to find his co-worker Trey to commiserate on their shitty work situation. He had tried convincing her to skip the party altogether, but Paige didn't want to miss out on the free food and drinks and the above average goodie bags.

She assumed Chance was becoming increasingly more disillusioned with his job than she was with hers—which was saying something. But she made a note of his unenthusiastic attitude, regardless. It wasn't like her boyfriend to be in a mood like this.

On her way to the bar she passed a custom ice sculpture of a snowman their CEO had created, a table stacked with goodie bags, and the door to the women's bathroom, which conveniently gave her a chance to reapply her lipstick and make sure her golden blonde hair was still holding a curl. Based on how lavish their parties always were, Paige would have thought she worked for a swanky corporate law firm, not Chicago's fourth-largest marketing agency.

She walked up to the bar at the same time as her counterpart, Brian. He was a nice guy, but Paige couldn't help but feel slight animosity toward him. Brian was hired after her and promoted before her, which wouldn't be a big deal if he actually had original ideas. But instead he just parroted what the online gurus were all doing and saying and got rewarded for it.

Thankfully, one of his work buddies sidled up next to him before she got trapped in another uncomfortable conversation, but she didn't want to risk anyone else cornering her alone at the bar, so she ordered the quickest drink—a glass of white wine—and ambled around the party in an attempt to find Chance.

Paige had started at the company right out of college in an entry-level marketing associate position, but in the last six years she had barely progressed like she had hoped. Paige felt so lucky at first to land this job, but it didn't take long for her to realize that, unlike her fantasies, marketing jobs weren't as sexy in real life as they were on TV.

Now she was twenty-eight, underappreciated, stuck with the most uninteresting accounts, and was often left out of meetings she felt she should have been included in.

Paige had finally gotten her first promotion at the beginning of this year, despite being the hardest worker and most innovative thinker on her team. Each time a new opportunity opened up in the past, the role went to guys like Brian or to new hires. Apparently, they finally decided to throw her a bone.

After her first three thankless years, Paige had polished up her resumé and geared up to go back on the job hunt. But then one morning she turned around from the coffee maker and walked right into Chance—the new hire in the IT department.

Chance was over six feet tall with brown curly hair. He wore glasses, but not in a nerdy way. It took less than two seconds of eye contact for Paige to forget about her plans to find a new job. She was instantly hooked on Chance.

At first, they took their coffee and lunch breaks together. Chance was an awkward type of funny that Paige found irresistibly charming. She started looking forward to work each day, brushing off her frustration at how she was being treated by her own team.

Soon enough, casual lunches turned into after-work drinks, which turned into attending concerts, which eventually led to Chance asking her out on an actual date. Paige could barely contain her excitement when she broke the news to her roommate and BFF, Nadia.

She and Chance became inseparable, spending workdays together and hanging out with Nadia and her boyfriend, Linus, on a regular basis. Chance stayed most nights at Paige's apartment, which she had purchased a year earlier with a generous inheritance check from her late grandfather that covered her down payment—one of the benefits of being the only child of an only child.

He was her first serious boyfriend, but Paige was sure they'd get married. After all, it was Chance who had said "I love you" first. He talked regularly about their future together, as if it were a given, which made Paige feel secure. Though when she brought up marriage, Chance always found a way to avoid the topic.

What had started out as a casual office romance quickly turned into a serious relationship.

Three years later, she and Chance were both still at the company, but it was getting harder and harder to ignore her dissatisfaction with her job—promotion or not.

And lately, Chance had been getting more fed up with his job, too. The company had been in the process of switching CRM systems so his team was slammed, not only with getting all of the systems updated, but also IT tickets from older employees who couldn't figure out how to navigate the new platform. It had put a big damper on his mood, both in and out of the office.

He had been putting in overtime at work and was spending fewer nights at Paige's apartment, and she couldn't help but feel it was starting to impact their relationship. He acted distant when they were together and irritated when she called to check in, but she figured it was all of the added stress that was getting to him. She was looking forward to the upcoming Christmas break so they could reconnect and get some much-needed quality time together.

Where is he? Paige thought to herself as she walked through yet another room at the party.

It was then that she heard his familiar voice from around the corner.

"Shit, man. I really screwed this up. I should probably tell her, don't you think?"

Paige paused before turning the corner into the room. *What is he talking about? Did he screw something up with the CRM migration?* His boss, Jana, ran a tight ship. She wouldn't take this news very well, especially since the team was already behind schedule.

"Dude, I don't envy you," she heard another man's voice say. It sounded like his counterpart, Trey. "If you think you can live with it on your conscience, just pretend like nothing happened. But it's up to you, man."

Yeah, must be some IT department drama.

"If I cheated on my girlfriend I don't know how I'd ever be able to look at her the same way again," Trey continued.

Cheated? Girlfriend? Paige felt like she was falling from an airplane, tumbling toward earth with nothing to catch her.

"What the hell is happening?" She didn't realize she had said the words out loud and that her legs had moved her forward into the room until she was standing face-to-face with a pale-faced Chance.

He looked like a deer caught in the headlights, and Paige immediately knew that whatever she heard next wouldn't be good.

"I'll leave you guys to it," Trey said awkwardly before backing away and out of sight.

Paige's hands were shaking enough to send some of the wine from her full glass over the edge.

"Paige, I—"

"What is going on, Chance?" she demanded. "That sounded super sketchy. Please tell me it isn't about what I think it is."

"Fuck," he groaned, rubbing his hands down his face. In their three years of dating, she had only seen him in a state like this once when his brand-new car had been rear-ended after a Cubs game.

"I slept with Diana."

Paige stared at him blankly, sure that she must have heard him incorrectly.

"You . . . slept with . . . Diana? Diana, the new employee on the finance team? Diana, the pretty twenty-two-year-old blonde who always has her oxford shirts unbuttoned just one button too low, Diana? Diana, the—"

"Yes, for Christ's sake. Yes, that Diana," he admitted in a near whisper. "Paige, I'm so sorry. I didn't mean for it to happen. We were both at the office working late one night and got to talking, and one thing led to another and . . . well, you know."

Paige felt like she had gotten slapped in the face. *Surely this is all a dream,* she thought. *Surely my boyfriend is not actually admitting to cheating on me with a twenty-two-year-old.*

Paige took a step backward, and her eyes were suddenly glued to the toes of Chance's dress shoes. "I can't believe this is happening."

"You have to believe me, Paige. I feel terrible. It was a one-time thing. I'm begging you to forgive me," he pleaded. Paige reluctantly raised her gaze to find that Chance's face was as white as a ghost and he looked like he was about to puke. His eyes were wide with fear.

She didn't have it in her to feel sorry for him.

"Are you freaking kidding me?" Paige snapped. "Chance, you can't cheat on your girlfriend of three years and expect her to just forgive and forget on a dime."

Her world was collapsing in on her. Just ten minutes ago, she was staring out over the cityscape and the worst thing she could imagine was getting stuck talking to Gerry about lizards. Now she was staring at the man she thought she would marry with the knowledge that he had betrayed her.

"I don't think I'll ever be able to trust you again."

She took a few more steps away from the man she barely recognized anymore, her vision blurring as tears welled in her eyes.

"Paige, please." Chance took a step toward her, but she batted away his arm and left the room, heading past the ice sculpture to the elevator, trying to remain undetected in the sea of her colleagues. Right before she reached the elevator, she stopped and turned around. Chance stood at the opposite end of the room, looking worse by the minute. But instead of closing the gap between them, she angrily snatched a goodie bag off the nearby table and pivoted back to the open elevator.

She didn't have the end of her relationship on her bingo card for the year, especially not right before Christmas. She was meant to be driving to Chance's family house in Wisconsin in a week to spend the holiday week with them. Instead, she had tears falling on her phone screen while she sat in the back of a cab and looked up last-minute flights to visit her family in San Diego.

Twenty minutes later she was unlocking the door to her apartment and falling into the arms of Nadia, who she had texted on the elevator ride down at LondonHouse. Nadia already had a bottle of wine with two glasses sitting on the coffee table and a Lindsay Lohan Christmas movie queued up as she led Paige toward the couch.

"So, should we slash Chance's tires first, or build up to that?" The expression on Nadia's face was both serious as shit and sympathetic as she lifted a wine glass in Paige's direction. Through her tears, she managed a smile and an eye roll.

"No need for violence." Paige sighed, plopping down next to Nadia. Instead of taking the glass from her hand, she reached for the full bottle on the table and settled into the couch.

Nadia slung her arm over Paige's shoulders and pulled her into a tight squeeze. "Good thing I brought two bottles."

Chapter 1

Eleven months later . . .

This is certainly not what the movies prepared me for,
Paige thought as she leaned back in her office chair.
She swiveled around and watched her gray cubicle blur
around her.

Paige grew up watching movies like *How to Lose a Guy
in 10 Days*, where the female lead character got to work
on marketing and advertising campaigns for a diamond
company. She saw big boardrooms with floor-to-ceiling
glass windows and corner offices with incredible views.

But just five minutes earlier, she had received an email
from her boss with information about her new client—a
local plumbing company whose brand was quite literally
in the shitter.

Sure, her office had fancy boardrooms, but she never got assigned the type of clients that were given catered meetings there. She was stuck in the cubicle farm and, even with her promotion nearly two years ago, still forced to work on the agency's C-list projects.

As her cubicle came back into focus, she stared at the photos pinned next to her computer. There was a picture of her with her parents at the top of Willis Tower, taken last summer. She looked equally like both of her parents. She had her dad's green eyes and pointed nose, and her mom's oval-shaped face and dirty blonde hair.

The other picture was of her and Nadia, her best friend and roommate. It was a photo from their trip to Nashville a few years ago. They had gone all out with the cowboy boots and bedazzled jean jackets. Neither of them had worn the boots since, but they made for a cute photo in the moment.

Paige was waiting to leave work to meet Nadia for a Pilates class, followed by their weekly Thursday sushi and reality TV night. Their current show was *Love is Blind.*

Nadia and her boyfriend, Linus, had gone on vacation for two weeks at the end of October, and the girls hadn't had much time to catch up on the trip or their TV shows, so Paige was looking forward to some uninterrupted bestie time.

Friends since high school, Paige and Nadia were practically inseparable. Not only were they roommates, but they also worked a couple of blocks away from each other, making it a no-brainer to meet up for after-work activities.

Paige looked at the time in the corner of her computer. She still had ten minutes to kill to ensure she wasn't leaving at the same time as Chance and Diana, a ridiculous practice she had gotten used to over the past eleven months.

After all the drama that happened with Chance last year, everyone expected her to leave the company. And the thing is that she absolutely wanted to, but on her own terms.

Paige dreamt of being able to build her own marketing consulting business and being her own boss, but she didn't want to quit after the breakup and have it look like she was trying to escape Chance or Diana.

Besides, she barely made a livable salary and had little savings to fall back on at that point—especially after buying the last-minute flights back to San Diego last Christmas. So she told herself back in January that she would stick it out one more year to give herself more of a cushion before branching out on her own.

Another twelve months of her salary plus the hefty end-of-year bonus the company always gave out would give her a more stable footing for freelance life.

That's not to say the last eleven months haven't been awkward as hell. In the days after last year's Christmas party, Chance apologized profusely and begged for another chance. He went on and on, swearing it was just a one-time thing, a stupid late-night slip. There was nothing between him and Diana, and it was a terrible mistake he wished he could take back.

It was far too soon for Paige to even consider forgiving him, and in more or less words she told him to fuck off. Chance was the guy she had pictured in her future, and his affair shattered everything she thought that future would look like.

And though it sounded dramatic, his confession shattered her favorite holiday too.

Paige had spent Christmas with her family in California to take some time and distance to process what had happened. But no matter how hard she tried, she couldn't get into the holiday spirit, which was a first for her.

As angry as she was at him, she couldn't help but miss him as she opened up her stocking on Christmas morning. They were supposed to be swapping stockings and gifts together at Chance's parents' house in Wisconsin, and being apart for the holiday gave her some new perspective.

When New Year's came around, she felt ready to sit down and talk with Chance about reconciling. She loved him, and even with this betrayal she felt like their relationship was worth a second chance.

She sent him a text right before her plane back to Chicago took off and switched on airplane mode. When she landed four hours later, she expected to see his grateful response, but only a welcome home text from Nadia came through. It wasn't until she was clicking through her Instagram stories that she saw posts from colleagues who had gotten together for a New Year's Eve party, with Chance and Diana cozying up in the corner sharing a midnight kiss.

Paige sunk into the airplane seat and replayed the story about ten times before finally believing what she had seen—Chance's deep regret for his actions apparently had an expiration date.

By the time everyone was back in the office a few days later, the gossip was buzzing, and Paige couldn't avoid the looks of pity being thrown her way no matter how hard she tried.

Meanwhile, Chance and Diana made no effort to hide their new relationship. It was like nothing changed at all for Chance. He took the same coffee breaks, ate his same turkey sandwich at lunch, but instead of doing these things with her—like he had for the last three years—it was Diana at his side.

Despite her heartbreak, Paige was determined to maintain her composure at the office and stay focused on her work just long enough to build up the savings she needed to leave it all behind.

And on days like today when she got assigned to a crappy client like this plumbing company, she couldn't help but check the countdown on her calendar to January, when she was planning to give her two-week notice. The company should be sending its end-of-year bonus email any day now. This is the email she was anxiously awaiting—the email that would give her an exact idea of how much of a cushion she could have for her freelance venture.

As much as she complained about her company and her below-average salary, they certainly gave out above-average bonuses each Christmas, in addition to their annual over-the-top and lavish holiday party. It was the single thing that had kept her going this past year.

Well, that and the support of her parents and Nadia.

It was twenty after five and time for Paige to make her way to the Pilates studio.

She glanced at her email one last time before shutting her laptop, packing up her purse and grabbing her gym bag.

***

"These guys are just saying what the girls want to hear," Nadia said with a mouth full of California roll. "Ten bucks says Josh has a girlfriend outside of the show."

The girls were sprawled out on their couch in their pajamas with three rolls of sushi and a carton of edamame on the coffee table in front of them. The Pilates class had kicked them in the butt and they weren't planning on moving the rest of the night.

"For a woman madly in love, you sure are a cynic when it comes to dating shows." Paige laughed.

"I mean, it's *because* of Linus I'm so judgmental!" Nadia said. "All these men just seem so childish and immature. Except Nate. Nate passes the test."

"Well, I'm sure Nate would be thrilled to know he made your cut. Do you think if you and Linus did this you would have picked each other?" Paige asked.

The premise of the show had always fascinated her. Singles meeting and getting to know each other behind a wall was certainly an interesting way to fall in love. But Paige wasn't sure she bought into love without physical attraction.

"Erm, I want to say yes, but as you remember it was my extreme beauty that made Linus come over and talk to us at the bar that night," Nadia said as she batted her eyelashes at Paige.

Paige had only a vague recollection of that evening, thanks to an extremely boozy Long Island Iced Tea. She and Nadia had been in Chicago for a year and a half and took advantage of the bars and clubs on most weekends. They were twenty-three, single, and not looking for anything serious. But everything changed that night.

The girls were standing at the far end of the bar, giggling as they brought up memories from their college escapades. Nadia had noticed the group of guys across the bar looking in their direction, pointing out the one with the glasses in the button-down.

To be fair, they were both looking pretty hot that night. Paige had gone for black jeans and a black leather jacket, which made her dirty blonde hair seem a bit more blonde than it really was. Meanwhile, Nadia had chosen a black miniskirt with a tight bodysuit—a look that accentuated her bigger-than-average boobs.

She had just gotten her jet-black hair cut into an above-the-shoulder bob and was wearing red lipstick. There was no way men weren't going to stare at her.

Sure enough, after twenty minutes of stolen glances, the cutie in the glasses found the nerve to walk up to her and ask her for her number. He had no weird pickup lines or gimmicks, just an old-school and arguably romantic approach.

And that is how Nadia met Linus Eriksson, her boyfriend of six years now, and honestly one of the best guys Paige could have chosen to date her lifelong best friend.

"Hey, Paige, speaking of Linus, I actually want to talk to you about something," Nadia said, lowering the volume on the TV. Her expression screamed, *I-hate-that-I'm-about-to-say-this.*

"Linus asked me to move in with him while we were on our trip last week. He's dropping major hints at a proposal over the holidays, and he really wants us to start building more of a life together," Nadia said, then exhaled loudly as if she'd been holding her breath.

Paige had known this conversation was imminent, but it didn't make it any easier to finally face the reality of their changing circumstances.

Nadia had been her roommate since freshman year of college. And since Paige was an only child, Nadia had become like a sister to her. Living with Nadia was comfortable and fun. She felt like home. And in this last year of heartbreak, having Nadia had been her saving grace.

Paige didn't quite know what to feel in this moment. There were so many mixed emotions. She was sad for herself because she would be losing the privilege of having her best friend living just down the hall. But she was genuinely happy for Nadia. Nadia loved Linus, and Linus loved her. They were so happy together, and after dating for six years, it didn't come as a shock to Paige that they were ready to take this next step in their relationship. She knew it was finally time for the sun to set on her and Nadia's roommate era.

And besides, Linus only lived a twenty-minute walk from her condo, so the move would hardly be taking Nadia away from her.

"Nads, I'm so, so happy for you! Truly." Paige wrapped her in a big hug. "When are you planning on moving out?"

Personal feelings aside, Paige did have a sinking feeling in her stomach. Nadia moving out meant she would lose her monthly rental payment, even if it wasn't all that much compared to other apartments in the area.

Paige started doing the mental math and figured that while she'd take a slight hit by covering the full mortgage payment, she should still have enough tucked away from last year's bonus and the upcoming holiday bonus to make ends meet and stay on course for quitting her job in January.

"Well, I know I already paid rent for November, but, uh, Linus wants me to move in this weekend."

"This weekend?!" Paige almost dropped the piece of sushi between her chopsticks. "So tonight is really the end of an era."

"I know, I'm sorry it's so quick, and please don't even think about sending back my November rent. Consider it my parting gift," Nadia said as she pulled Paige back into a hug. "Ugh, I'm gonna miss you!"

"The feeling is mutual," Paige replied, a lump forming in her throat. "Promise we can still continue our cozy Christmas traditions?"

One of the things that made the girls such great friends and roommates was their similar taste in just about everything—including cheesy Christmas movies and over-the-top decorating. Even after Chance's Christmastime confession last year had dampened Paige's holiday spirit, Nadia pulled out all the stops to bring back her cheer.

"Oh, please. If you think Linus is about to sit down for a five-hour Christmas movie marathon featuring only Lacey Chabert, then you've lost your mind," Nadia said. "Keep plenty of popcorn and hot chocolate with the mini marshmallows stocked in the condo."

Paige laughed at the mental image of Linus in an ugly Christmas sweater lounging on the couch watching predictable Christmas rom-coms. And she was comforted by the confirmation that her best friend really wasn't going anywhere.

Chapter 2

P aige spent most of Friday afternoon at work scrolling through old photos of her and Nadia on her phone and Facebook account.

She wanted to find the perfect pictures to use in her congrats gift for the big move.

Paige had the idea of creating a custom label she could wrap around a bottle of wine. She was putting together a collage of their best roommate moments to print out at work and tape on the bottle she had gone out to grab at lunch. The girls were meeting for happy hour after work to have one last roommate hurrah before Nadia started packing up.

Earlier in the day, she had taken more time to revisit her budget and evaluate her bank account to see just how much impact Nadia's departure would have on her goals. She had to replace her washer and dryer in August, which did a number on her savings. Right now, she had enough to make it three months without an income while she started seeking clients. But when she factored in the cost to buy a new laptop, it teetered closer to two months.

The bonus check from her company would hopefully buy her extra time to get her business more established. She wasn't sure she was willing to take the risk without this extra cushion.

Paige glanced at the time on her computer. It was just past four now, and she figured she should probably wrap up her wine label project and attend to actual work before the end of the day.

She clicked over to her email tab and saw a company-wide message from the CEO, sent just two minutes before, with the subject line: *Update on Holiday Bonuses.*

This was the email Paige had been waiting for, and she opened it immediately.

Her excitement was short-lived, and her stomach sank as soon as she started reading the first line.

Due to unexpected financial challenges, we will be unable to give out bonuses this year.

"This can't be happening," Paige grumbled to her computer screen while rereading the message again to make sure she hadn't imagined it. But after her fourth time through, she realized that the floor had indeed fallen out from under her.

She could hear the whispers from colleagues around the office as everyone read the email. She definitely wasn't the only one who was pissed.

How could this be? She thought. *The company is getting a consistent stream of new clients. Are they mishandling their finances that badly? Sure, their Christmas parties are always over-the-top, and when A-list clients come in for meetings they splurge on catering, but surely they wouldn't be doing those things if money was tight. Right?*

No amount of speculation could change the fact that she wasn't getting her bonus—the bonus that motivated her to stick it out at a shitty job where her ex and his new girlfriend worked for *a year.*

How could I have been so stupid to rely on this?

Her mind kept spinning and running the numbers from that morning again.

The lack of a bonus on its own was devastating, but on the heels of Nadia's move-out notice it was downright catastrophic.

In addition to losing the daily routine she loved with her best friend, her financial situation just went to shit, and her plans for quitting and going freelance were now on an indefinite pause.

As much as she wanted to leave her job, she wasn't willing to do so without a realistic financial safety net.

Paige sat in her cubicle with her head in her hands. She had always prided herself on being an optimistic person who could take blows in stride. Supporting evidence being the fact that she stuck it out at her awful job while her ex paraded around with his new girlfriend like their breakup didn't phase him at all.

But the last twenty-four hours felt like one bomb after another, leaving nothing but wreckage behind.

She did her best to regain her composure and think through her options.

Option one, I just stay put and continue to stash what I can from my abysmal paycheck. And heck, maybe another promotion will come up. Hmm, can't bank on that. Option two, I polish up my resumé and start applying elsewhere like I should have done four years ago. But nooooo, stupid Chance had to show up and distract me from leaving. This isn't the worst idea, but the application and interview process could take a while, meaning I'll be stuck here regardless. Plus, it's always a risk working in corporate. Who knows what other companies might be like. Could they be worse than here? Okay, option thre–

Paige's phone chimed next to her. It was Nadia.

> Hey! Just heading out of the office. I'll head to Cruz and grab us a table.

Paige checked the time, sent her photo collage document to the printer, and gathered her things. *What better way to numb the shock than with a margarita . . . or five*, she thought.

Plus, Nadia was the type of friend who was always in your corner. She'd know exactly how to cheer Paige up.

> Packing up now. Oh, and order a pitcher.

***

"Oh good, the pitcher is already here," Paige groaned as she slid into the chair across from Nadia, pouring herself a full glass.

"Your message made it sound like a code red, so there are also chips and queso and guac on the way," Nadia said. "So, what's going on? Did you get passed over for another promotion? Did they assign you a new client from hell?"

Nadia never missed a beat. After more than fifteen years of friendship, she knew how to read between the lines of Paige's messages.

Paige proceeded to fill her best friend in on the last hour, showing her the email all the employees received.

"Oh, screw them!" shouted Nadia across the table. "Those bonuses are the only ounce of appreciation they ever show you. Ten bucks says they are still giving pay raises to the top executives. Who are all men, I might add."

Knowing the pricks that ran the company, she probably wasn't wrong.

"What am I going to do, Nads? I'm so done there. I keep getting the bottom-of-the-barrel clients, and lately it feels like Chance and Diana have upped their office PDA, if that is even possible. I think if I stay there much longer I will actually go insane," Paige said. "You know I've been itching to do my own thing, but I just can't get myself to go through with it if I don't have a safety net."

She finished the entirety of her first margarita and poured herself a second, following it up by stuffing a chip topped with guacamole in her mouth.

"I know, Paige. I'm so sorry you have to deal with this," Nadia said. "I can't help but feel like my announcement last night makes it all worse."

Paige reached over and squeezed her friend's hand. Nadia had done so much for her over the years—especially in the wake of her breakup. And as much as Paige wished Nadia wasn't moving out, she knew it was time for Nadia to take the next step in her relationship.

"Nadia," Paige finally spoke. "Nothing you do or say could *ever* make my life worse. It's long overdue for you and Linus to live together. I will be fine, just after I complain over a few margaritas." She clinked her glass against Nadia's and took a big sip.

"And besides," she continued, "I barely charged you rent. Your continuing to live there wouldn't have really made a big enough difference."

It was true. Paige felt weird collecting a massive rent check from her best friend—she only asked for half of her mortgage payment so they paid equally.

"Wait a minute. Paige, you just gave me an idea!" Nadia said, perking up. "You are—I guess *were*—barely charging me to rent out your second bedroom. With me out of the picture, you can charge a new roommate *way* more and actually save some cash. We are in a great neighborhood, and your place is way nicer than half of the places that pop up in rental Facebook groups. You have a cash cow!"

Nadia had a point. Paige hadn't even considered this as an option when she was spiraling in the pit of doom . . . well, her cubicle.

She was perfectly content splitting her mortgage payment if it meant Nadia was in the room across the hall, so she'd never considered how much money she could make from properly renting the room out.

An hour ago, the news about not getting a bonus felt like a knockout blow after an already tough week. Now, Nadia was painting a clearer picture of how she could stay on track to making her dreams a reality.

Nadia continued, "I can help this move along ASAP. I'm already planning on getting my things moved over to

Linus's this weekend, so I can help spruce up the place for some photos so you can start bringing in the mon-nay."

Paige wasn't sure if her newfound optimism was warranted or if it was just the margaritas talking, but she had a good feeling about this new plan.

"Well, it seems that we need another round to celebrate!" Paige said after using the last of the first pitcher to top off their drinks. "To your next adventure in love, and my padded savings account."

"I can certainly drink to that." Nadia looked around to get the server's attention, pointing at the empty pitcher.

Chapter 3

Paige's head was pounding when she woke up on Saturday morning.

Did I forget to drink water last night? The closer I get to thirty, the crappier I feel after drinking, she thought.

She heard rustling outside in the kitchen, meaning Nadia must be up and packing.

Paige hoisted herself out of bed, grabbed a sweater from her closet, and downed the full glass of water that was still sitting on her bedside table.

"Morning," Paige groaned as she walked out into the common area. "Packing already?"

"There she is!" Nadia called. Her whole body was practically inside the kitchen cabinet rummaging for something. "Yeah, I'm just doing a sweep of the kitchen to make sure I didn't miss anything."

She emerged from inside the cabinet with a cutting board and a party platter dish she had painted at a pottery studio back in their college days and put them in a box that was half full.

It was strange for Paige to see all of Nadia's things sitting together in the box. It made the fact that she was moving out all too real.

"I can't believe you're packing up," Paige said solemnly. "I've never lived as an adult without you."

"Stop it, Paige, you're gonna make me cry." Nadia's lip quivered.

But it was the truth. They had been friends for over fifteen years, and they'd lived together for eleven of them. It was shocking they still hadn't tired of each other.

Nadia was Paige's best friend, her soul sister, and their friendship was the thing she treasured most. For years it had been them against the world.

In high school they bonded over their shared love for boy bands, the *Twilight* books, and the so-bad-they're-good teen dramas on TV. It's no wonder they spent hours each holiday season on the couch watching predictably cheesy Christmas movies.

They both stayed local and went to college at San Diego State University and didn't have to think twice about rooming with each other.

During college, they partied and hooked up with cute boys, but at the end of the day they were always each other's priority. No guy ever trumped their friendship.

As they approached graduation, Paige had an itch to get out of San Diego and live a bigger city life, and thankfully Nadia felt the same way.

They considered San Francisco, New York, and Boston, but looking at rental prices online made their wallets hurt. So, when they started looking into Chicago, it felt like the perfect balance of a big city while still being semi-affordable.

They sent in more job applications than they thought was even possible, and within a couple of months they each had something lined up in the Windy City.

Paige and Nadia took Chicago by storm with adventurous and wild spirits. There were new restaurants to try, new bars and clubs to check out, and plenty of men to meet. But like their college days, they each kept things casual, prioritizing their friendship above all else.

And then about a year after the move, Nadia met Linus, a sensible Swedish-American boy who grew up in the suburbs of Chicago. He adored Nadia and made her already bright light sparkle even brighter.

They dated casually at first, but it quickly developed into something that Paige could tell was serious. And while she was overjoyed that her best friend had found her match, there was a dull sting that their time as a dynamic duo was coming to a close.

Sure, Paige had a couple of work friends who were fun to hang out with, but no one could ever match Nadia. She was the real deal when it came to friends, and Paige was going to miss having her so close.

"What are you doing?" Paige asked as Nadia karate chopped the pillows on the couch.

"Oh, I'm just tidying up for some photos," Nadia replied. "And trying to distract myself from crying."

Paige could see her friend's eyes were glassy. Nadia wasn't a big crier, so it was clear this was an emotional morning for the both of them.

"Nadia, don't worry about straightening up, you have enough to do today."

"Don't be silly, Paige. I've already packed up my closet, decorations, and knick-knacks, and taken quite a few boxes over to Linus's earlier this week," Nadia said. "All that's left is the furniture, which is yours."

The girls peered into Nadia's room. There was a queen bed and mattress stripped of the bedding, a dresser and desk with bare surfaces, and a closet with empty hangers.

"It looks so weird without all of your things." Paige sniffled.

"I know," Nadia said, her voice echoing in the empty bedroom.

The friends looked at each other, fighting the urge to break down in tears right then and there.

"There's no time for tears!" Nadia exclaimed as she pushed past Paige to grab her iPhone. "We have pictures to take, and we can't forget I'm only a twenty-minute walk away."

That seemed to be the point both girls were forgetting. Linus's apartment was a closer walk than Target. Still, it didn't make the separation as roommates less painful.

Nadia snapped photos from every possible angle of the bedroom, the recently tidied up living room, the kitchen, and the laundry unit.

"I'll AirDrop these to you. Give me your phone." Nadia grabbed Paige's phone without waiting for a response. "I've also taken the liberty of writing out a post for you to put in the Facebook groups."

Paige rolled her eyes and laughed. Nadia was always the "mom" friend out of the two of them. It wasn't surprising she had basically taken care of the entire roommate search.

Even with the groundwork taken care of by Nadia, Paige still had some apprehensions about making the post.

"What if my new roommate sucks? What if I only get weirdos reaching out to me?"

"There's always going to be weirdos out there. But I have no doubt you'll get some good options. It's Chicago. People are moving here all the time."

Nadia always knew the right thing to say. Something Paige was going to miss having access to 24/7.

"You're right. I just want to get someone in here quickly so I can start putting money away," Paige said. The more she thought about getting a new roommate, the more relieved she was to have a plan to make up for the lack of bonus—and then some.

"Don't worry, I'll help you write up questions to ask in your interviews to help you weed out the bad eggs and find someone *almost* as good as me," Nadia said with a grin.

"All right," said Paige. "Let's find me a roommate before Christmas!"

***

By Sunday evening, Paige had received quite a few messages about the open room. The unfortunate thing was that most of these messages came from obvious scammers, people asking for a rental price even less than Nadia had paid, or couples looking to share the room.

In reality, Paige had about five qualified leads, so she started sending messages to set up interviews.

Within a few hours she had three interviews set up and two messages back from girls who had already found somewhere else.

Damn, she thought. *That was quick.*

The first two interviews were set up for Tuesday at a Starbucks around the corner from Paige's office. Based on her Facebook message conversations, they both seemed promising.

The first interview was with Ariel. She was a transplant from LA, not far from Paige's family in San Diego. She worked in environmental law, and according to what she could see on Facebook, seemed to enjoy living a healthy lifestyle. *That will be good*, Paige thought. *Maybe I'll pick up some healthier habits.*

The second interview was with Wren, an early twenty-something who, she learned from their short yet information-packed exchange, lived most of her life in the Chicago area but had spent the last year traveling around Europe. *Perfect, someone to give me travel advice once I start making better money.*

Paige was optimistic that by the end of Tuesday she'd have a new roommate lined up, and one that she would enjoy living with.

***

As soon as her eleven o'clock Tuesday meeting let out, Paige grabbed her purse and headed around the block to meet Ariel, her first roommate interview. She walked into Starbucks and was immediately hit with a smell that didn't belong indoors.

She saw a young woman standing a few feet inside the door in coveralls, wearing her hair—which looked a bit greasy—in a messy bun.

"Ariel?"

Paige hoped the woman wouldn't turn around.

"Oh, hi! You must be Paige. It's so wonderful to meet you in person."

Ariel was about as granola as they come. Apparently she took her environmental duties to the extreme, and Paige judged based on the greasy hair alone that she only showered once every two weeks.

This is totally fine, she told herself, *you can look past this. Think about all the money you'll save!*

When they reached the barista, Ariel ordered a latte with oat milk. Paige opted for a regular vanilla latte. The girls made some small talk about the colder weather and their jobs while they waited for their drinks and then found an open table near the entrance.

"I'm glad we were able to meet and talk through the possible living arrangement," Ariel said.

"Yeah, me too. I wa—"

"I noticed you ordered a latte with regular milk?" Ariel interrupted. "It's fine because this is our first official meetup, but I'm a strict vegan and can't live anywhere that has any animal byproducts in the kitchen."

Paige almost spit out the sip of dairy-filled latte she had just taken.

Surely Ariel was joking? This had to be her way of breaking the ice. Or was she actually serious about controlling the kind of food she bought for the house?

Taking a chance, Paige smiled and said, "Haha good one! Very convincing."

"Oh, I'm not joking." Ariel was quick to defend her original statement. Maybe Paige shouldn't be so surprised. After all, given Ariel's apparent shower routine—or lack thereof—it seemed clear she was serious about the environment, if not personal hygiene.

"Not only is eating animals inhumane, it's killing our environment. I can't be part of a household that contributes to this climate disaster."

Okay, so cross Ariel off the list. Paige was all for combating climate change, and she could even be convinced to have vegan meals once or twice a week. But this level of control was too extreme for her liking. She had to pull the plug on this one.

"Ariel, while I admire the cause, it's just not going to work out for me," Paige said. "I hope you can understand that I'm going to need to go in a different direction with the roommate search."

She tried her best to look sympathetic and not as if she were talking to an insane person.

"Suit yourself." Ariel shrugged her shoulders and looked only slightly annoyed by Paige's statement. "I hope you can sleep at night knowing you're destroying the world."

And with that, Ariel got up and exited the café, leaving Paige dumbfounded at their exchange.

As soon as Ariel was out of sight, Paige picked up her phone to call Nadia. She could barely get through the story without laughing.

"Wow, you really dodged a bullet there," said, joining in Paige's laughter. "When is the next meetup?"

"Wren will be here in twenty minutes. But she seems totally normal, so I have a good feeling about it."

The friends said a quick goodbye before Nadia went into a meeting and Paige checked her Facebook post for more comments before Wren arrived—just in case she wasn't as normal as her messages led on.

There weren't any other promising leads, so Paige crossed her fingers this next interview would go off without a hitch.

Just like she could smell Ariel before seeing her, Paige could hear Wren before looking up and seeing her standing at the door.

Well, she could hear Wren's dog, that is.

Wren stood just inside the doorway in a matching Lululemon sweatsuit set, carrying a Louis Vuitton bag on one arm and holding a small poodle—who hadn't stopped barking since she walked in—in the other.

She caught Paige's eye and made her way toward the table.

"Paige?! I'm Wren! Soooo great to meet you, girl!"

"Wren, hi! And who is this?" Paige nodded at the poodle, who had thankfully quieted down now that Wren was seated.

"Oh, this is Noodles, my service dog," Wren said with a wink.

As if on cue, Noodles began yapping at a man who walked past the table, then looked toward the door and barked at the two women who had just walked in. *Some service dog*, she thought.

Paige hadn't really considered a roommate who might want to bring a pet with them. And as much as she loved dogs, Noodles wasn't making a great first impression. She did her best to ignore him.

"So, Wren, you spent some time traveling?" Paige was eager to get to know more about her potential roommate. "What's next for you?"

"Let me tell you, if you haven't been to Europe, you *have* to go. I can't even order a coffee at Starbucks anymore after being exposed to *real* coffee in Italy. And don't even get me started on the croissants."

It took everything in Paige's power not to let out a snort at the way she used an exaggerated French accent on the last word.

"I bet," Paige replied. "I have never be—"

Yap, yap, yap.

Noodles was at it again, this time staring down the toddler who sat two tables away.

"Oh, Noodles, will you just hush!" Wren said in a tone that didn't seem to catch Noodles' attention in the slightest. She set him down next to her feet out of eyeshot from the toddler.

"He's just the cutest little thing, isn't he?" Wren was clearly oblivious to the fact that her dog was annoying every other person in the room.

And then it happened.

The smell hit her nose first, then Paige could feel all eyes of the patrons at Starbucks staring at their table.

This can't be what I think it is, right? Paige thought to herself. She forced herself to look down.

Sure enough, right next to Paige's foot was a fresh poop, courtesy of Noodles.

"Noodles! You are so naughty!" Again, Wren's tone with Noodles had no sense of frustration or command.

"No matter how hard I try, he just can't seem to get potty trained," Wren said with almost a laugh in her voice, sealing her fate in the roommate interview.

Maybe Paige could have gotten past the annoying barking—after all, it couldn't possibly be happening all day,
right?—but she absolutely could not get on board with a
dog who was going to relieve itself in her home.

Wren grabbed one of her poop bags, cleaned the mess,
and handed Paige the leash.

"You don't mind holding on to Noodles while I toss
this, do you?" She walked away before Paige could even
answer, but instead of heading toward the door to the
street, where there was a trash can conveniently next to
the café, Wren headed straight to the trash can at the
stand next to the counter with the napkins and sugar
packets and threw the poop bag in.

It took everything in Paige to pick her jaw up from the
floor. Was she being punked? Were there hidden cameras
somewhere? Because this meeting was only going from
bad to worse.

Thinking quickly, she stood up as soon as Wren got
back to the table.

"Wren, I'm so sorry, I'm needed back at work for an
emergency. I'm afraid I need to go!" Paige lied through
her teeth. "It was great to meet you—and Noodles—and
I'll let you know about the room."

Paige wasn't necessarily afraid of confrontation, but
she did not want to be associated with Wren and Noodles
any longer than she needed to be.

"No problem, girl!" Wren replied, completely unfazed by the past five minutes. "We'll look out for a text from you!" She finished her sentence with a wink, holding up Noodles and making a wave motion with his paw.

And with that, Paige hurried out of the Starbucks with secondhand embarrassment and no roommate prospects.

Chapter 4

"Nadia, I'm telling you it was awful. Imagine the horror stories you read about bad dates. That is exactly what this was like. She didn't even bat an eye at the fact that her dog took a shit inside a Starbucks. And not to mention her *service* dog," Paige said, rolling her eyes and then imitating the wink Wren had given her.

She had just gotten home from work and FaceTimed Nadia to fill her in on her tragic second interview.

I know it's only Tuesday, but do you want to come over tonight and order sushi and watch *Love is Blind*?" Paige made sure to sound desperate. "I think Jeremy and Kylie are going to have that fight they've been teasing over the last few episodes."

After a miserable day, all Paige wanted to do was curl up on the couch, stuff her face with imitation crab and rice, and watch the shit hit the fan for other people.

"I can't tonight, Paige. I told Linus we could finish unpacking my things. All my boxes are starting to drive him crazy."

"Fiiiiine." Paige sighed. "More edamame for me then."

They spent a few more minutes catching up on Nadia's workday until Linus popped on the screen to whisk Nadia away to do their chores. After hanging up, Paige sat back on the couch, listening to the silence that flooded the apartment.

It was weird having things so quiet. She and Nadia had lived together for so long, she had gotten used to constant background noise. But now, Paige was alone with her own thoughts.

She couldn't quite identify what she was feeling. But she had been sensing it creeping in the back of her mind for a while now—growing stronger with the sudden silence.

With all the quiet, Paige realized that while Nadia and Linus included her in just about everything they did together, she had become more and more lonely this past year.

Since high school, Paige had always had someone all to herself. First it was Nadia. Then Chance. And while Nadia had always been there, it wasn't the same with more of her focus shifting toward Linus.

Sure, they still had plenty of solo girls' nights when they were roommates, but now instead of swapping miserable dating and hookup stories like they used to in their college and early Chicago days, Nadia shared frustrations that come with a six-year relationship, and Paige shared excuses for not going on any dates at all.

Dating had been fun and casual when they first moved to Chicago and she and Nadia were both doing it. But once Nadia got serious with Linus, it left Paige to be the only one looking for a one-off fun time, or with the pressure to actually find Mr. Right.

And she thought she had with Chance. Until he decided to get in bed with the blonde new hire.

Paige hadn't dated at all since the breakup. She couldn't help being afraid to open up to someone knowing that person had the ability to shatter her heart again.

Logically, she didn't want to be with Chance anymore. He cheated on her, came crawling back to her promising it meant nothing, and then after a week of being alone, decided he might as well start dating the girl he cheated with.

He sucked. She knew it. And Nadia knew it even before Paige did.

It didn't take long after Chance's Christmas party confession for Nadia to tell Paige how she *really* felt about her new ex.

As much as Paige had planned double dates, the couples never quite jived the way she had wanted. But she was blinded by her love and infatuation for Chance, so she always shook off the lukewarm feelings from all parties.

But once Chance was out of the picture for good, Nadia didn't shy away from letting Paige know she thought he was a loser with little ambition and a bland personality. And Paige couldn't help but agree.

Still, as much as her logical brain knew it was for the best that the relationship was over, she had been crushed in the weeks and months that followed Chance and Diana's office debut. Seeing the man she believed she would marry walk hand-in-hand through the office with a new girlfriend made her question everything about the validity of their relationship. Had he even cared about her at all? It hurt her to see how much it looked like he wasn't hurting.

So, dating had been off the table.

She told herself she was fine on her own. She still had Nadia as a roommate and best friend, and Linus was always kind, warm, and thoughtful towards her. But as she sat in the empty apartment, she realized maybe she was lonelier than she thought.

Should I download the apps? She thought to herself. *It's been almost a year now . . .*

As she switched the TV on to watch Netflix, an automatic preview for *Too Hot to Handle* started playing. Paige couldn't help but stare a bit too intently at the handsome shirtless men with washboard abs that flashed on the screen.

She clicked on it, and while the intro played, she went to the app store on her phone, searched for Hinge, and hit download.

***

The following days had Paige feeling hopeful.

She had some newfound confidence after spending some time swiping on the dating apps and receiving some flirty messages.

But while she had been scanning through Chicago's dating pool, she had received another message in the housing Facebook group from a promising lead.

Her name was Allison, and she had been living in Chicago for a few years, originally from somewhere in southern Illinois. Her lease at her current house was about to be up, and she said she was ready for a change of scenery. The big plus was that she worked as an engineer at a tech company and didn't scoff at the price.

No forceful diet restrictions, check. No pets, check. Has the funds to pay the rent, check. *Allison just might be the one*, Paige thought.

They set up a time to meet on Thursday during their lunch break, and Paige woke up that morning with an optimistic feeling that this would be the day she found her roommate.

Allison arrived on time, smiling and politely shaking Paige's hand. Paige had suggested the same Starbucks she met with the other roommate prospects hoping none of the employees would remember her from the day of Noodles' incident.

"It's so great to meet you," Paige said before the girls joined the line for a coffee.

Allison looked—and smelled—normal, and as far as Paige could tell, she didn't have any surprise toy poodles hiding in her purse.

After a few minutes of small talk while they were waiting for their drinks, they found an empty table and got into house details.

"The building is great—not too old, nice amenities, and the handymen I've found are quick to fix anything that happens," Paige said proudly. "So," she continued, "tell me a little more about your routine and living style."

She sipped her coffee, waiting anxiously to confirm that Allison was indeed as good a roommate choice as she hoped she'd be.

"Yeah, I'd be happy to," Allison replied. "I am in the office every day from about eight to five. I try to cook most dinners at home and then pack a lunch each day before work. I'm very tidy and clean my dishes almost immediately after using them. I'm used to splitting house chores, but don't mind doing some extra cleanup if it's needed."

Paige couldn't believe what she was hearing. Was Allison the perfect roommate? She was tidier than Paige was, check. She cooked, which would help her save money, check. There were no red flags in sight.

"Well, it sounds like a great match so far!" Paige couldn't keep the smile off her face. "So, your current lease is up. Are your housemates just not renewing? Are they all moving out too?"

"Oh no, they are all staying. But I just had to get out of there." Allison appeared to shudder just thinking about it.

"Yikes, they're that bad, huh?" Paige asked, awaiting the juicy details.

"There are three other girls and they are just super annoying. It's like, every morning before work they stand around the kitchen recapping *Love is Blind* or some other crappy TV show."

Paige's face went pale, and she looked down at her coffee cup to try and avoid eye contact. She didn't want her facial expression to give away the fact that she was a major consumer of reality TV.

"Like, can't I just make my lunch for the day in peace without hearing about who kissed who and who is causing all this made-up pointless drama?" Allison seemed truly irritated by the idea.

Paige didn't know what to think or say in response. How many evenings and mornings did she and Nadia spend talking about which men from their favorite reality dating show were the hottest, or about the petty things the women on the show did to stir the pot? And don't even get her started on all their other "crappy" TV shows, as Allison had called them.

Was this a deal-breaker? Paige supposed she could cut back on the reality TV nights and see if she could convince Linus to let her and Nadia watch their Hallmark Christmas movies at his place instead.

It could work! She told herself. She just needed a few months of extra income, after all. Surely, she could survive a six or twelve-month lease with limited trash TV.

"Well, yeah, that sounds like a frustrating situation!" Paige finally said, hoping Allison couldn't see through her forced response. "You'll be way more comfortable in a new place."

"Exactly! That's why I was so happy to see your listing pop up. It's perfect, and I'm totally fine with starting on a six-month lease."

Phew. She could make it six months if she had to.

After a little more small talk and showing off some photos of the apartment, Paige said goodbye to Allison and walked back to her office. Her mind was swirling with thoughts.

Was she really okay with packing away the parts of life she enjoyed just to appease a potential roommate? But on the other hand, was she okay with losing out on thousands of dollars because she wanted to watch hot guys run around on the beach trying to impress girls who were out of their league?

Just as she returned to her desk, her phone vibrated in her pocket. She found another Facebook message on her screen with another interested renter. A man.

She opened the message:

> Hey. Looking for a nice space ASAP. Willing to pay above the asking price and can move in quickly. I'm 30 years old, work in finance here in Chicago, and spend most days and evenings out, so I don't plan to be around much. Lmk. - Carter

Well, hi, Carter, Paige thought as she spied his profile picture—a close-up shot of a gorgeous, tan, and smiling man with dark-brown hair. Even from the small circle she could tell he was handsome. *What are these apps and dating shows doing to me?* Paige hadn't been this thirsty in a while.

Focus, Paige.

She hadn't really pictured her new roommate being male, but this guy seemed almost perfect. He hadn't scoffed at the rental price, he wouldn't be around much to complain about her TV watching habits, and he was definitely easy on the eyes.

She typed back:

> Hey, Carter! Thanks for reaching out! Are you able to meet at five today around LaSalle and Erie? I can send you the address for a Starbucks there. We can chat through some details.

Within minutes, he replied with, "Sure," and Paige couldn't help but smile at her phone screen.

Once she snapped back to reality, she wished she had suggested meeting up the following day so she could have planned a cuter outfit. She was wearing an oversized tan blazer over a fitted black tee with black pants and chunky black loafers. It wasn't her most exciting or flattering outfit, but it was going to have to do.

He's a potential roommate, Paige. Not a date.

Unable to focus on her work, she clicked on Carter's profile image to do some light stalking.

Private, of course. She rolled her eyes.

But there were three photos set to public that she could see.

One was a photo he had been tagged in, clearly from the late '90s. She guessed he must be around nine or ten years old in this photo. He was in a loose baseball jersey with a gap between his front teeth, posing next to a guy that could be his dad. A cute picture, but not what she was hoping to find.

The second photo was a professional shot of a men's high school lacrosse team. She scanned the image and found a guy who could be a sixteen-year-old Carter standing in the back row. *So, he's tall then*, she made a mental note.

The third photo wiped the smile off of Paige's face. It was Carter and a brown-haired woman on a boat at sunset. The woman was giving him a kiss on the cheek, and while the backlighting kept Paige from seeing her face clearly, she could tell this woman could be a model.

Well, not surprised a man this hot might have a girlfriend. But then why is he looking for a roommate? And why is he considering a female roommate? Either this man is fresh out of a breakup or he is extremely bad at updating his Facebook page. Both are equally possible.

If Carter was post-breakup, Paige had no interest in being a rebound. And if he did have a girlfriend, then he was completely off-limits. Only a year ago she was the woman who was cheated on—she could never be the other woman.

But there wasn't enough information on Carter's barren Facebook profile to be sure. For all she knew, this photo could be from 2018 and he's been single for six years.

Paige pretended to work, and as hard as she tried not to let her mind wander, she came up with different scenarios of how she and Carter might fall in love—or at the very least fall into bed.

The end of the day couldn't come fast enough.

***

Five o'clock rolled around and Carter was nowhere in sight. Paige checked her watch every five minutes, becoming increasingly annoyed at his tardiness and lack of response to her "Hey, I'm here" message. Luckily, she had a book stashed in her work bag to occupy the time while she waited for him at Starbucks.

Forty minutes passed and still nothing. Paige had tried making up excuses for him for the first twenty minutes, but by the time thirty minutes, then forty came around she was starting to feel steam come out of her ears. Sure, his profile picture was hot, but standing up a potential landlord for a roommate interview with no communication was downright rude.

Just as she was packing up to leave, Carter finally waltzed in the front door with a stony look on his face. He was wearing an expensive-looking gray overcoat with a white Oxford shirt and tailored navy-blue pants. His dark-brown hair was longer on the top but held in place perfectly by product. He looked like he had walked out of a J.Crew catalog, but that didn't erase the annoyance Paige felt.

"Hey! I've been waiting for you," Paige said with a sour tone.

"Yeah, my bad," he replied without an ounce of regret or apology. He even had the gall to look down at his watch as if he had somewhere else to be.

Carter looked like a Greek god, chiseled by Michelangelo himself, but all Paige was feeling in that moment was rage.

How could he be so inconsiderate? Doesn't he need something from me?

"I already have a drink, are you going to grab something?" Paige gestured to her now lukewarm hot chocolate.

"Nah, I'm good," he said coolly with a look on his face that said he'd rather be anywhere else. "So, let me get down to it," Carter started. "I'm in a situation where I need to move out quickly, and I just need somewhere on a month-to-month basis while I find new arrangements. Ideally, I'm looking for somewhere in the Lincoln Park neighborhood that looks nice, and where I feel comfortable crashing at night. I don't plan on spending much free time at the apartment with work and social events. And oh," he added, "if there are other offers, I'm willing to pay more."

This got Paige's attention. And given the fact that Carter was already on her nerves, she decided to take advantage of his last statement. *Let's squeeze this guy for all he's worth.*

"Actually, I did meet with a few people yesterday and today, and two of them are serious about the room and ready to sign a lease. But if you're willing to pay five hundred more each month I'll send you a lease tonight, and you can start moving things in as soon as tomorrow."

She stared him down, using all of her power to look confident and unwavering in her negotiation.

"That's fine," said Carter. His tone was the same as when he first walked in, like the thought of being in this Starbucks meeting was a waste of his time.

"Great, then it's a deal." Paige stretched out her hand to him to shake on it, but Carter reached for his phone and started texting someone instead of acknowledging her.

The nerve of this guy! I should have asked for more than five hundred extra.

"I'll send over my phone number, email, and other details in a message. I gotta go."

And with that, Carter got up and left the café. Paige was stunned. A few hours ago she was dreaming up fantasies about falling in love with her handsome roommate. Now she could barely stand knowing they'd be sleeping under the same roof. But at least she'd be raking in more money at his expense. Plus, he was good with a month-to-month lease, which gave her more flexibility to kick him out once she saved up enough.

On her way home she called Nadia to debrief on the second day of interviews.

"Wait, wait, wait, she is moving out because her room-mates talk about reality dating shows in the morning before work?"

It sounded even crazier when Nadia repeated it back to Paige.

"I know, Nads, it took everything in my power to keep my jaw off the floor."

"I mean, I don't even think we could count how many mornings we've had that exact conversation." Nadia could barely get the sentence out without laughing. She added, "It's definitely in your best interest to tell her no! That is borderline psychotic to be that irritated by something so normal."

Then Paige started on Carter, sparing no details about his rude behavior.

"Nooooooo," said Nadia. "Paige, you are not telling me that the hottest man in Chicago wants to live in your place for *more* money than you listed it for." Paige had texted Nadia a screenshot of Carter's profile photo, which Paige had to admit didn't do him justice.

"He is such a prick, Nadia! He was rude and not even sorry for being forty minutes late without a single message. And then he dissed my handshake!"

"Not the handshake!" Nadia repeated.

"I tried to do some sleuthing and I guess there is a chance he is fresh out of a breakup, which could explain his moodiness, but I'm not sure I can let that slide as an excuse."

"I mean, newly single or not, the guy is clearly not boyfriend material, and it sounds like he will just keep to himself and not engage with you. So, it will essentially be like living alone . . . just with some nice eye candy every now and then."

"I can't argue with the logic, but he was a total jerk!" Paige griped.

"I say you suck it up and then eventually hate-bang him."

Paige had to push the image out of her mind before it distracted her.

"Nadia! I'm hanging up the phone immediately."

"No, don't!" Nadia begged. "I'm sorry, I'm sorry. He's just so hot. And you could really use a good roll around in the bedroom after your nearly year-long dry spell."

"Oh my god, now I'm really hanging up," Paige said as she hit the red button to end the call.

Nadia wasn't wrong. Paige had avoided dating and hookups ever since the breakup. As much as she wanted to get revenge on Chance after he cheated, she was too sad after it all happened. And by the time the sadness faded away, she was scared any rejection would reopen the wound.

She immediately had a text from Nadia:

> I'm sorry! I support you with whoever you choose ;)

Paige sighed and wrote back:

> Well, you'll be happy to know I'm sending him the lease as soon as I get home.

She looked down at Nadia's filthy emoji-filled reply and couldn't help but blush.

Carter was hot, yes. But there was no redeeming his personality. They would just be roommates, nothing more.

It took the rest of her walk home to finally stop blushing.

An hour later, after careful deliberation, she caved and sent a message to Carter confirming the room was his and that he could move in over the weekend. She attached a lease she had made using an online template that included general rules for the apartment, their agreed-upon price, and her Venmo information.

After just a few minutes, a notification popped up on her phone. It was a single thumbs-up emoji from Carter.

Really? She thought. *How cocky and arrogant do you need to be to include zero words of thanks or excitement to your new roommate?*

But Paige barely had time to scoff at his response, because shortly after the thumbs-up message, she had another notification from Venmo with Carter's first month of rent. She transferred the money to her bank account and couldn't stop smiling as she cracked open her laptop and started working on her business plan.

Chapter 5

C arter had moved in his things by Saturday afternoon—speaking as few words to Paige as he could.

Aside from a gruff "hello" and "is it okay to leave the car parked there?" he silently brought in his few boxes with AirPods in his ears and what looked to be a slight scowl.

It was a true shame Paige couldn't ignore his sour attitude and poor manners, because damn was Carter nice to look at.

Even though they were halfway through November, his skin was still tanned—an olive complexion worthy of the red carpet. His jawline was strong and accentuated by a neatly trimmed stubble, something Chance was never able to grow. On Thursday his dark hair had been slicked back for a more professional look, but today he had some curled strands falling down around his eyes, giving him an added boyish charm. His look was more casual than

at their meeting on Thursday, and Paige hated how well
he pulled off both looks.

He wore a Lululemon shirt that hugged his biceps,
and as he reached for a box at the top of the stack near
the doorway, she couldn't help but see a six-pack hiding
underneath.

Because why wouldn't he have washboard abs?

Paige immediately turned on her heel and went for a
glass of water.

She hated that a man this annoying could be so hot.
Maybe that's why she tried starting another conversation
with him.

"So," Paige said at a volume loud enough to penetrate
the AirPods, "not that many boxes I see. You ditch all
your belongings to run from the mob or something?"

She gestured her elbow into the air next to her as if she
were knocking it into someone's shoulder.

Carter must have barely heard her because he glanced
in her direction with a confused and annoyed look on his
face as he took out his right earbud.

"What?"

"Oh, um, I just said it doesn't look like you brought
much with you and asked if you were hiding from the
mob," she said, noting it was definitely less funny the
second time around.

Carter didn't say anything. He stared at her as if she had
just said the Earth was flat. Finally, he rolled his eyes and

said, "Not that it's your business, but I only brought what I needed for a temporary stay. Storage units are a thing, you know."

And with that he put his earbud back in, grabbed a box, and retreated into his room.

Paige could feel her skin getting hot again. *This guy is the actual worst.* But she shook off her frustration, remembering it was only temporary.

She grabbed her laptop and started studying other marketing freelancer websites and LinkedIn pages so she could have a good idea of how to position herself when she quit her job in a couple of months.

Later that night, Paige decided to give Carter the benefit of the doubt, so she went out to buy some beers and frozen pizzas from the grocery store to extend one last olive branch.

So far, their interactions had been at the end of a workday and in the middle of moving into the apartment. Paige couldn't count on one hand the number of stressful days she had had in the office. Perhaps that Thursday they met up had been packed full of meetings that could have been emails. And Paige hated unpacking after a brief weekend vacation—so moving and unpacking into her apartment had been torture.

Maybe she was judging him too harshly given the circumstances of both times they'd been around each other.

Paige walked up to his door and knocked. Nothing. She knocked again. Still nothing.

Just as she lifted her fist to knock a third time, the door swung open.

"Yeah?" Carter asked, the scowl still present on his stupidly handsome face.

"Okay, hi to you too. I just wanted to let you know I got some beers and pizzas to welcome you to the apartment if you want to join me for dinner in twenty minutes?"

"No, thanks," he said cooly and started closing the door.

Paige stood dumbfounded by his response and instinctively put her hand out to stop the door.

"Are you serious? I'm just trying to be a good friend here. You're not even going to try to act polite?"

He stared at her again before answering, "I'm not here to make any friends. I just need a place to live for a while—preferably a place where everyone minds their own business."

And with that, Carter closed the door in Paige's face.

What. A. Prick.

Paige could hardly believe anyone could be this off-putting, but lo-and-behold here was the man to prove her wrong.

***

Days passed and Paige barely saw Carter—a fact she mostly appreciated.

He left quietly for work each morning and often returned around nine or ten in the evening and went directly to his room without any effort in speaking a word to her. Was it really so hard to say good morning? Would it kill him to fake a smile as he headed out the door?

Although she could have sworn she noticed him checking her out the morning she wore her I-have-a-client-meeting dress. It wasn't often Paige's bottom-tier clients came into the office for an in-person meeting, but when they did, she made sure to wear her most flattering girl-boss outfit.

But as much as she didn't want to interact with him, she didn't hate her new roommate's lingering glance.

And it would be a lie if she said she didn't return the favor. Every time she laid eyes on Carter he looked so fine.

Most mornings he left in a suit, and in the evenings he'd either return in casual business attire or joggers and a T-shirt if he was coming from the gym. Unlike the saying, she *did* love to see him go, because that meant she didn't have to deal with his arrogance. But she also had to admit she loved to watch him walk away.

For the first time in a long time, Paige was acutely aware of how she looked at home. She and Nadia had never minded looking frumpy when it was just them, but now with Carter's presence in the apartment, Paige thought twice about going braless.

And it wasn't even that she felt she *had* to change her at-home style. It's more that she found herself *wanting* to.

What is Carter doing to me? She caught herself glancing at herself for an extra two seconds in her bathroom mirror.

On Thursday night, Nadia came over for dinner and the *Love is Blind* finale, hoping to spot her replacement in the flesh.

"I can't wait to see if Mr. Hollywood lives up to his profile picture," Nadia teased from the couch, her first glass of wine almost empty.

"Trust me, the handsome effect wears off real quick once you exchange five words with him." Paige rolled her eyes, partly because she truly disliked him, and partly to try to convince herself that she wasn't still attracted to him.

"Honestly," Paige continued, "it's really not that bad of a setup. It's pretty much like living alone . . . I'm just getting paid for it. He is never here. I've actually never even seen him open the refrigerator. I'm not sure he eats!"

"That explains the abs you were drooling over last weekend." Nadia winked.

Paige had obviously filled Nadia in on Carter's move-in weekend, from his arrogance to his washboard abs.

"I was not *drooling* over them. I simply noticed them, burned the image into my memory forever, and texted you immediately to update you about said image of abs."

"Whatever helps you sleep, or er, not sleep at night," Nadia said with a little shoulder shimmy. "Okay, enough about Carter. How have the apps been going?"

After downloading the dating apps, Paige had solicited Nadia's help in creating her profile.

"Well, it started out strong, but then quickly went downhill. So far I've gotten at least fifteen 'What u doing later?' messages, seven requests for my Snapchat username, and one unsolicited dick pic. So, I'd say par for the course!"

"Oh god," Nadia groaned. "Where have all the good men gone?" She dramatically tilted her head back with the back of her hand to her head.

"You're telling me! You should be extra grateful for Linus tonight after you see the mess that is dating apps in Chicago. Sure, there are some normal guys on there, but no one who really . . . stands out."

"You mean there's no one as hot as Carter?" Nadia couldn't hide her smile as she said it.

"Oh my god, Nadia, don't you dare bring him back into this!" But Paige had to admit there was some truth to what Nadia had said.

"I kid, I kid. I just want you to be happy, and most of all I want you to be getting some while you're still young."

Paige stared at Nadia blankly from across the couch before throwing a pillow at her face.

"Careful with the wine, Paige! And speaking of wine, I need a top-up."

Nadia jumped up from the couch and made her way to the kitchen counter to where the open bottle was waiting and started pouring, while Paige opened up one of the dating apps on her phone to see if there had been any major changes since the last time she checked.

"Oh!" Paige gasped, looking down at her phone.

"OMG, what?" Nadia inquired, rushing back to the couch as fast as she could with a full wine glass.

"I matched with a guy named John a couple days ago and he's just messaged me asking to go out on a date tomorrow night."

Nadia snatched the phone out of Paige's hands within seconds.

"Okay, John." Nadia whistled. "He dresses well, has a good smile, and looks buff as hell. Pretty hot for a bald guy."

Nadia started typing while mouthing out, *"I'd love to! Name the time and place ;)"*

"Nadia! What are you doing? Give it back!"

"Too late! Already hit send." Nadia locked the phone and tossed it back to Paige. "This is good for you, Paige. It's time to get back on the horse. You're growing cobwebs *down there*."

Nadia pointed below Paige's waist without apology.

"Wowwww. You are the worst."

Paige knew Nadia was right. It had been ages since she had hooked up with a guy, and she was starting to wonder if she'd even remember how to flirt.

"That's what best friends are for, babe. If I don't nudge you back out into the dating world, no one will."

"Fine. One date. But I don—" Paige's phone screen lit up. "He just wrote back."

> Sunda in the West Loop at 7:30. Looking forward to it :)

Paige couldn't help but blush. She was going on a proper date, which was more than Chance had been doing for her near the end.

He was the king of "let's just order takeout" and put on a movie at home. Which Paige didn't mind now and then, but she had hoped her boyfriend would put at least some effort into wooing her.

"All right," Nadia said. "Now that we've settled things with your love life, we can get back to the train wreck that is this season of *Love is Blind*."

The girls ate sushi on the couch, downed the rest of the wine, and watched as the drama unfolded on TV.

Just shy of ten o'clock, the door opened and Carter walked in.

Nadia hit pause and leapt off of the couch to intercept him.

"Hi! You must be Carter, I'm Nadia, I used to live here," she said in one giant breath.

"Hi," Carter said, keeping it short as always and taking a side step to get around Nadia.

"So, Paige tells me you're a busy guy! What is it that you do?"

Carter turned around just as he reached the door to his room. "I've had a long day. If it's all right with you, I'm going to skip the chitchat and turn in for the evening."

And without waiting for her response, he entered his room and shut the door behind him.

Wow, Nadia mouthed as she turned back to where Paige sat on the couch, making her way back to her usual spot.

"Now you see what I've been dealing with," said Paige.

"I mean, yeah, he's not the friendliest, but like, WOW is that man gorgeous."

"After an interaction like that, the only thing you take away is how attractive he is?"

"How can you not? Paige, you need to go to the doctor and get your eyes checked. Maybe you aren't seeing what I'm seeing," Nadia said with a wink.

Oh no, I'm definitely seeing it. But unfortunately for me, his looks are overshadowed by his personality, she thought, not wanting to give Nadia the satisfaction of knowing she agreed.

"Like I said," Paige countered, "he keeps to himself and I'm basically living on my own while getting a nice monthly check. As long as I don't need to engage with him, I'm perfectly fine with how things are."

"Suit yourself," said Nadia as she hit play and settled back into the couch.

Chapter 6

"Tell. Me. Everything!" Nadia demanded the second Paige answered her FaceTime call.

Paige was still in bed but had her phone propped up on a pillow. She was groggy enough that she would probably drop her phone on her face if she tried to hold it.

She had gone on her date with John the night before, and apparently Nadia had taken her *"I'll fill you in in the morning"* text a bit too literally.

"I mean, it was definitely a one-time thing," Paige said. "He was nice and all, but just *so* boring. I felt like I was the only one asking any questions. It was like pulling teeth to keep the conversation going."

Paige had been both nervous and excited about the date. She spent most of the workday on Friday mentally choosing her outfit, eventually landing on an emerald cowl neck top with tight, faux black leather pants. She and John both arrived on time, and he was a perfect gentleman the entire night, which put her more at ease. But she was bummed about how much she had to carry their conversation. It wasn't easy like it had been right from the start with Chance. And as nice as he was, she had gotten a bit irritated by the end of the date at how much more effort she was putting in to getting to know him with nothing in return.

"Ugh, I hate that." Nadia sighed.

"But the confusing thing is that he texted me after we parted ways saying he had a great time and would love to see me again. Like, what? You're telling me our dull as hell conversation was a great time for you? Did we go on the same date?"

"Yeah, that's ridiculous," Nadia said. "What a bummer, though. He was very cute. But I'm proud of you for going. Hopefully boring baldie doesn't scare you off from going on more dates."

"You have too much energy for a Saturday morning." Paige laughed. She wished she could be doing her date debrief in person with Nadia as her roommate, but this FaceTime was a nice reminder that not much was really changing about their friendship.

"Linus made me a fancy latte. Blame him."

"Ooh, coffee is a great idea. I'm gonna force myself out of bed to make a cup. I'll text you later."

Paige got up and pulled on a sweater. She redid her bun so she wouldn't look like she had just rolled out of bed ten seconds ago, and wiped the remnants of her mascara that was smudged under her eyes.

She opened her door and was shocked to find Carter sitting at the kitchen island with a coffee from the café down the block, scrolling on his phone.

"Good morning," Paige said, more out of habit, not because she meant it.

"Yo." Carter didn't even bother to look up at her.

Well, at least this morning I get the decency of a two-letter reply instead of zero.

Paige figured she would take advantage of Carter's seemingly neutral mood.

"So, Thanksgiving is this week. Will you be here? Or are you going out of town?" Paige asked. "Because if you're staying here, you're welcome to join me and my—"

"I'm going out of town," Carter said, cutting her off.

"Cool," Paige replied. "Super cool."

She opened her mouth to ask him a follow-up question only to see him get up and turn to go back toward his room.

"Something wrong with the kitchen?" Paige asked sarcastically.

"Just prefer to have my coffee in peace," Carter replied with a smirk.

Really?!

Did he really think he could get away with patronizing her like that? She couldn't hold it in anymore.

"Why are you so freaking *rude*?"

The look in Carter's eyes told her he was enjoying the rise he got out of her.

"Look, Paige, I told you I'm not here to make friends and play house. I just need a nice place to crash, and this seemed to fit the bill."

He took another step in the direction of his room and then turned back around.

"Oh, and by the way, hope you enjoyed Sunda last night." He stared at her with another smirk on his face.

"What? How did you kn–"

"I was sitting at the bar when you walked in. Green is a nice color on you," Carter said before retreating to his room and closing the door.

Oh my god, he noticed my outfit? Paige thought. *Wait, don't let his compliment distract you. He's awful, remember?*

Paige almost forgot why she'd come out of her room, but she made her way to the Nespresso machine to get her coffee fix.

But as she waited for the machine, she couldn't help thinking about the fact that her hot as hell roommate had been secretly checking her out from the bar last night.

***

The next few days were more of the same with Carter. Just their regular hallway pass-by where neither of them really acknowledged the other.

After Carter's Saturday morning confession, there had been hardly any interaction between them, and each time Paige saw him, he looked increasingly grumpier.

She was glad to avoid his moody attitude, but there was a small part of her that longed for a sliver of his attention—a fact she would never admit to Nadia. After the confirmation that he had eyed her from across the restaurant, she found herself craving his stare.

Thanksgiving, which was one of Paige's favorite weeks of the year, was just a day away and the exact distraction she needed from this unwanted Carter craving.

Paige loved all holidays, and while Christmas took the top spot, Thanksgiving was close behind it. In the first couple of years after she and Nadia moved to Chicago, they traveled back to San Diego for both Thanksgiving and Christmas, which was fun, but very expensive for their entry-level salaries.

So, eventually, Paige and Nadia decided to stay put for Thanksgiving and create a week full of traditions for themselves to ease the sting of not going home. The first years were tough, but now they both looked forward to their week of festivities.

Wednesday was always their food prep day—getting dishes ready for Thanksgiving Day so they could spend Thursday focusing solely on the turkey.

Thursday was their Friendsgiving party for any and all of the Chicago transplants they knew who couldn't make it back to their hometowns for the holiday. And on Thursday night, the girls would put an air mattress out in the living room with tons of blankets and pillows and have a Hallmark Christmas movie marathon sleepover.

Friday was Paige's favorite day. She and Nadia would wake up at the crack of dawn to go Black Friday shopping at the big department stores on Michigan Ave to take advantage of the deals. Sure, most companies were starting their sales early and online, but there was something about the rush and atmosphere of the stores that gave the friends a holiday high.

After their shopping spree, they'd spend the entire afternoon decorating their apartment. Paige and Nadia had spent years—and admittedly too much money—collecting holiday decor to make the condo feel like you stepped onto a Christmas movie set.

For Paige, Christmas was the most magical time of the year, and she was mesmerized by the snow, pine trees, and cozy knitwear. Growing up in southern California, she'd only ever experienced sunny sixty-degree weather, palm trees, and hardly ever needed more than a light jacket.

She'd watch the classic Christmas movies like *Home Alone*, *Elf*, and *The Santa Claus* and wish that she could experience a white Christmas—just once. She remembered writing "Santa" multiple letters a year with updates on her good behavior, each time only asking for one thing: snow on Christmas morning.

Despite the California climate, her family would decorate the house as if they lived at the North Pole, and it was a tradition Paige was determined to keep once she was in her own place.

When she moved to Chicago, she finally got to experience snow for the first time, and it was just as magical as she'd hoped it would be. Now her decked-out Christmas interior matched the snowy exterior outside her window.

After Chance's affair the year before, her Christmas had been ruined. So, this year she and Nadia were determined to bring her Christmas cheer back. This meant they were going to go extra hard with their decorating.

Paige was getting the kitchen ready for Nadia's arrival with all their Thanksgiving groceries when Carter walked out of his room with a suitcase.

"Oh, hi. Leaving today?" Paige asked, not expecting a response.

"Hey. Yeah, heading to my mom's house for Thanksgiving," Carter replied.

Holy crap. I actually got a full sentence this time.

"Nice. Where does your mom live?"

"Just outside Philly."

"Nice," said Paige.

"Do you know any words other than 'nice'?" Carter's eyes narrowed in on her with a playful stare.

Paige felt her cheeks start to fire up.

"Why do you have to ruin every conversation we have?"

"I don't see how I'm ruining anything." Carter's tone was borderline sarcastic, his mouth curling up into a smile that could get anyone out of jail.

Damn, she really hated how good-looking he was. Almost as much as she hated how much she loved him looking at her.

"Well," Paige started, "enjoy your trip and tell your parents to have a *nice* Thanksgiving." She winked as she said it, waiting for any sort of reaction from Carter.

A wink?? What is this power hot men have over women, she wondered.

When he finally reacted, it wasn't what she was expecting.

Instead of making that smile even bigger, it fell flat, and his expression shifted into a pained look she had never seen on his face before.

But as quickly as the emotion appeared, it passed, and he was back to looking bored at being in the kitchen with her.

"So, yeah, I'm gonna go," Carter said, breaking the silence.

"Nice, I mean, cool. Yeah, sounds good. See you later," Paige replied awkwardly.

As he turned to walk toward the door, Paige could have sworn she saw his mouth curl back up into a smile.

He opened the door to find Nadia standing with enough groceries to feed a small army. Without offering to help, he stepped around her and headed to where his Uber was waiting on the street.

Real classy, Carter.

Any of the butterflies Paige had felt at the sight of Carter's smile quickly flew away.

"So, I take it Grumpy isn't joining tomorrow?" Nadia quipped as they hauled all the bags inside.

"Nope, but I did just have a conversation with him that lasted more than ten seconds," Paige said, unable to keep a smile from creeping up on her face.

"OMG, and??!! Why are you smiling??"

"Settle down! Trust me, it's not nearly as juicy as you want it to be. As par for the course, he ended up making fun of something I said, which got me all flustered. But I think he *enjoys* making me mad. Like there is some sick obsession with getting a reaction out of me. Because, Nadia, the smile on his face . . ."

Paige's mind drifted off to the mental picture she had taken of his face just minutes earlier.

"Earth to horny Paige," Nadia said, her voice interrupting the thought.

"Ugh. Why does he have to be so freaking dreamy?"

"Because you have literal cobwebs in your vagina, that's why! Which is exactly why you need to give the apps another chance. Clearly you have . . . needs . . . that aren't being met. And it seems you want Carter to meet them."

There was no way Paige was going to let Nadia know this was exactly what she wanted.

"I could not look at myself in the mirror if I let myself stoop so low to sleep with a guy who is that rude and narcissistic with no remorse for how he speaks to people."

"Easy. Just cover up the mirrors," Nadia smirked.

Paige rolled her eyes before continuing, "It *was* weird, though. I told him to tell his parents happy Thanksgiving, and for a second he had this look on his face. Like I had told him his puppy died or something."

"Odd. I'm assuming he didn't say anything?"

"Nope. Went right back to looking like he'd rather be anywhere else but in my presence."

"That's the Carter we know and love," Nadia said sarcastically. "I'm sure he's just keeping his distance because it's a temporary arrangement, or because he is recently single and heartbroken, or because he's a man in a woman's apartment and doesn't want to come across as creepy. Sure, he could be a little warmer, but if you put yourself in his shoes, he's probably just trying to keep a respectful boundary."

"Yeah, I guess? Whatever, it doesn't matter. I'm hoping it's only a few months before I can kick him and his moodiness out," Paige said, thinking about the cash she could store away with Carter's rent payment.

"Get that money, girl," Nadia chimed, changing the subject back to their Thanksgiving agenda. "Okay, I say we start with the homemade stuffing since that takes a while. And then we can move on to the creamed corn."

"Yes, chef!" Paige held her hand up in a salute and got to work unpacking the bread.

Chapter 7

T hanksgiving went off without a hitch.

The meal, in all of its many courses and side dishes, was delicious as always. This year, their Friendsgiving included Paige's colleague Laura, Nadia's colleague Jason and his boyfriend Kyle, plus Linus and his childhood friend Mike. The day provided lots of laughs, which kept Carter far from Paige's thoughts.

She and Nadia had just returned from their Black Friday shopping spree, which ended up being more window shopping than actual shopping. But Nadia had nabbed a cashmere sweater that was on sale for Linus's mom, leather gloves for his dad, and a candle and trinket dish for his sister.

Paige had already told her parents that her presence would have to suffice as their main present this year, but she took advantage of the bookstore's buy one get one fifty percent off deal and got them each a book so she wouldn't be completely empty-handed on Christmas morning.

Now it was time for their favorite part of the day: decorating.

Each year, Paige and Nadia surprised each other with a new holiday-themed sweater to wear while they were decorating. It was always so hard for Paige to keep her sweater a secret, but the grand debut after they returned from their Black Friday hunt was a highlight of the day.

This year, Paige found an oversized knit cream sweater with embroidered Christmas-themed items scattered over the front and back. Nadia showcased a sweatshirt with actual blinking Christmas lights.

Once they were in their cozy decorating uniforms, with Mariah Carey singing them in, they got to work putting up the tree—a fake one, but the kind that makes it almost impossible to tell—followed by Christmas lights and their shared collection of kitschy ornaments. After the tree was done, they filled the rest of the condo with wreaths, nutcrackers, festive pillows, tea towels, vintage Santa salt-and-pepper shakers, Christmas candles, chunky knit stockings, more small trees, garland, and tinsel.

Hours later, every surface was covered in holiday cheer, and Paige and Nadia sat on the couch with Christmas-themed mugs filled with extra boozy hot chocolate and gooey marshmallows, proudly surveying their hard work before Nadia had to go home to her new apartment.

"When is Carter coming back?" Nadia asked as she got up to start packing her bag.

Oh, right, Carter. Paige realized she had barely thought about him while he was gone with everything she had going on.

"I didn't ask." Paige shrugged. "I'm assuming tomorrow or Sunday."

She was exhausted from their three-day holiday extravaganza and couldn't wait to pop on another Christmas movie and fall asleep.

She opened Instagram while Nadia packed, and her stomach dropped. The first post in her feed showed Chance down on one knee proposing to Diana, with the caption: "*I have so much to be thankful for this year. She said yes!*"

It hadn't even been a year.

She knew she should just keep scrolling, but she couldn't look away. Paige couldn't stop looking at the way Chance was beaming at the gorgeous blonde girl. She couldn't remember him looking at her like that in any of their own photos.

And, because why not add insult to injury, she swiped through the carousel of photos and confirmed that this was indeed the largest rock she'd seen on a non-celebrity engagement ring.

How did he afford that? She wondered. *Anytime I brought up getting engaged, he always had some excuse lined up about not having enough money saved up to get me the ring I deserved. But apparently his wallet is just as loose as his behavior was when it came to Diana.*

Paige knew she should have unfollowed Chance after the breakup, but there was a part of her that needed to know if this assumed fling with Diana was more than just an office hookup. And with each month that passed, his Instagram stories featured more and more coffee dates, kisses in front of The Bean, walking hand-in-hand on Navy Pier, and summer getaways to his parents' lake house in Wisconsin—a place she had only been invited to once in their three years of dating.

She hadn't wanted to get back together with him. But she'd silently hoped the day would come when Diana would end things and he'd finally experience the heartbreak she had felt last December.

Seeing the engagement post shouldn't be a shock. They didn't try to hide the fact that they were serious around the office. But the finality of it felt like a punch in the gut.

Chance was living his life as if nothing had ever happened. He continued being in a relationship, only swapping one blonde for another that was five years younger.

And now, here she was nearing thirty years old with no dating prospects, a roommate who barely even acknowledges her existence, a job that doesn't value her, and a joke of a savings account.

"Paige." She barely registered her friend's voice.

"Paige," Nadia repeated. "What's going on? What's wrong?"

It wasn't until then that Paige felt tears streaming down her cheeks. She turned her phone screen toward Nadia, who dropped her bag immediately and rushed to hug Paige after seeing the picture. It only made Paige cry harder.

"That motherfu—" Nadia started before getting distracted by the sound of a key in the front door.

Carter.

Startled, Paige turned away from the door, not wanting Carter to notice her red, splotchy, mascara-smudged face.

He walked inside and his face hardened the second he noticed the updated decor.

"What the hell is all of this?" Carter said, less as a question and more as an angry observation, clearly not picking up on the mood of the room.

"Well, obviously it's Christmas decorations." Nadia didn't bother to hide her annoyance. "We're actually in the middle of—"

"Take it down," he interrupted, each word biting the tense air between them. "This looks insane. I live here too, you know. And I refuse to look at these absurd decorations for the next god only knows how long."

Nadia turned to face him, shielding Paige from view.

"Calm down, dude."

Carter was fuming now.

"If I remember correctly, I pay for half of the condo. So that means I get a say in how my half looks."

Before he even finished the sentence, he grabbed one of the empty boxes near the storage closet and made his way over to the bookshelf near his bedroom door. He began grabbing the candles, tinsel, and all other Christmas decorations in his path and placed them back in the box.

Until he reached the couch and noticed Paige.

Paige saw his eyes widen with awareness, but Carter didn't back down. Instead, he proceeded to the right half of the living room and filled the rest of the box.

"Okay, Carter." Paige rose from the couch to face him, feeling the liquid courage from the extra shot of vanilla vodka she put in her hot chocolate. "Quit being an asshole. This is childish behavior."

"Well, these decorations are childish," he responded, holding up a pillow with the words "Holiday Who-be-What-ee?" on it, which was, appropriately, a quote from *How the Grinch Stole Christmas*.

"What does it even matter to you? It's not like you've ever bothered to spend time here," Paige said, face turning even redder. "Has it occurred to you that maybe the world doesn't revolve around you and that this is some-thing that makes people happy? Or are you too much of a grinch to care?"

"You don't have to be a grinch to be put off by these tacky Christmas decorations," he retaliated.

I can't believe this is happening, Paige thought. *This has to be a nightmare.*

Carter's behavior on top of Chance's engagement an-nouncement was enough to push Paige over the edge.

"Well, if you don't like them, then move! You clearly hate it here, so just find somewhere else to live!"

"Fine," Carter said, leaving the now full box of decora-tions next to the Christmas tree. "Here, do whatever you want. I'll start looking for something new this weekend."

And with that, he walked back to where he had left his suitcase and proceeded to close himself in his room.

The girls stood there in silence for what felt like an eternity before Nadia grabbed the vanilla vodka from the counter and poured them each a shot.

"Well, shit," Paige groaned as she sank back into the couch. She had barely even tasted the shot as it went down her throat.

"I don't know what the hell his problem is," Nadia said as she followed suit. "But it seems like Mr. Grinch's heart is three sizes too small. I wonder how big that makes his di—"

"Nadia," Paige cut her friend off before she could finish.

"Too soon? I had a feeling, but I just couldn't help myself."

Paige buried her face in the pillow and let the last ten minutes sink in.

Chance is engaged. And Carter is a big enough asshole that I actually kicked him out. Paige felt sick, and not just from the alcohol.

The realization hit her hard: as soon as Carter leaves the apartment, her cash flow and freelance dream will leave with him.

Leaving Chance to officially win their breakup, once and for all.

***

Saturday came and went with no Carter sightings—something Paige was grateful for, especially given her intense hangover. She had gone a bit overboard with the vanilla vodka after the drama on Friday night.

She wasn't sure what she was going to say to Carter when she saw him next. He was out of line for being so demanding about the Christmas decorations, which she had promptly put back in their places on Saturday morning. And he had definitely noticed her crying and continued in his Scrooge-level tirade anyway.

But there was a part of her that felt embarrassed about her reaction that night. Carter had only lived with her for two weeks, and she basically kicked him out with the snap of a finger. Did unfriendliness really warrant an eviction notice?

And that's not to mention the fact that Carter had seen her in complete disarray. As sick as she was of being around him, Paige was still conscious of the fact that he was an attractive male who she hoped thought she was attractive in return.

She wasn't sure her red, splotchy face and puffy eyes did her any favors in that department.

But today, Carter was the least of her concerns.

Today, Paige had to focus on how she was going to get through the workday tomorrow. It was going to be the first day back after the holiday, which meant Chance and Diana would be parading around her massive ring and telling their engagement story to anyone who would listen.

Paige wished she could just take a sick day to avoid it all, but she didn't want to look like she couldn't handle it. So, since it was Sunday, she planned on having a self-care day to ensure she walked into the office tomorrow looking bright-eyed and bushy-tailed with freshly painted nails and an outfit that screamed, "*I'm completely unfazed by my ex getting engaged to the girl he cheated on me with less than one year after the scandal in question.*"

She texted Nadia, and within twenty minutes Paige was on her way to meet her best friend back on Michigan Avenue to take advantage of the lingering Black Friday deals.

Chapter 8

M onday morning started with Paige and Carter walking out of their rooms at the same time and heading toward the kitchen.

It was their first run-in since Friday night's dramatic decoration outburst.

They both stood awkwardly on opposite sides of the counter before Carter spoke. "Hey, so I'm going to be starting my apartment hunt. Given the time of year, I'm not sure how quickly I'll find something. At least not as quickly as I found this place."

Silence fell between them, and Paige maintained eye contact with Carter, refusing to offer him the apology she assumed he was fishing for. At the very least, he seemed to hope she would take back what she said about him leaving.

The truth was, Paige didn't *want* to find another roommate. Carter was paying a premium price she wasn't sure others could match, and who knew how many weirdos she'd need to sift through again. But Paige was stubborn and didn't want to be the first to apologize, so she simply replied, "Sounds good."

Their eyes stayed locked on each other, daring the other to fold first. But Paige also saw a flicker in Carter's eyes that she had glimpsed before. A sadness of sorts. He looked like he was about to say something more but must have decided against it because he turned without another word and left the apartment.

"Okay, bye," Paige called out to the empty room, rolling her eyes at his abrupt departure. She made herself a coffee and mentally prepared for the day.

When Paige made it to her office, she opened the group chat she had with her closest colleagues—Jenny and Laura from the graphic design department—and asked them if the coast was clear.

Paige had spent a few hours the day before going back and forth with her coworkers on a plan of action. Luckily, Jenny enjoyed getting to the office early to get some work in while it was quiet, so that meant she could be Paige's eyes and ears on the inside so she didn't walk directly into the happy couple.

Jenny wrote back:

> All clear. I don't think they've gotten here yet.

Paige rushed into a closing elevator to find Trey standing nervously next to the buttons. Trey was Chance's counterpart on the IT team, and the friend Chance had confided in at the office party after he cheated. He gave her an awkward smile but avoided any direct eye contact.

Off to a great start, Paige told herself. But as soon as the elevator door opened, she held her head high and made her way to her desk.

She could feel just about everyone's eyes on her, giving her looks of pity, but Paige kept her focus on acting cool, calm, and collected as she walked through the cubicles.

After checking her email and doing some prep for a last-minute team meeting, Paige headed for the coffee station. Before she turned the corner into the break room, she could hear Diana's voice gushing to the HR team.

Paige froze. She craved a caffeine fix, but certainly not enough to barge in on Diana's engagement recap. As if on cue, Laura walked out with two coffees in hand, handing one to Paige.

"My hero," Paige said as her entire body relaxed slightly.

"I walked by while you had your eyes glued to your computer and noticed you didn't have any yet." Laura smiled, ushering Paige away from her blonde nemesis.

The rest of the day was thankfully incident free, and Paige was exhausted from the constant awareness of her surroundings in addition to the boring team meeting and uninteresting client work.

In the days and months that followed her and Chance's breakup, she wasn't able to avoid him completely. But each time they had a run-in, she was able to walk off before he had a chance to try to explain himself or ask how she was doing. She knew that eventually she would pass him in the hallway and need to give him a forced and empty congratulations. She just hoped it wouldn't have to be today.

Jenny and Laura had both left for the day, and Paige had waited her usual twenty minutes past five to ensure she was one of the last people to leave the office. She made her way to the elevator and hit the button for the lobby. Just as the doors were closing, an arm shot between them, forcing them back open.

Seconds later, Chance stepped into the elevator.

Paige felt like the wind was knocked out of her. *You have got to be kidding me*, she thought.

"Oh, hey, Paige," Chance said awkwardly, hitting the button again. Paige stared straight at the doors.

After a few seconds of painful silence, Chance turned toward her like he was about to speak just as the elevator landed with a thud in the lobby. The doors opened, and

Paige made a beeline to the door, leaving her ex to choke on his words.

Her mind was spinning her entire commute home, thinking of all the things she wished she had said to him in their brief encounter. She also felt the pain of his nonchalance resurface again and did her best to fight back tears on the train.

As soon as she got back home, she collapsed on her couch and covered her head with a pillow. Without thinking, she started screaming into the pillow to let off some steam. While she was mid-yell, she heard the door open and sat up so fast she got dizzy.

Carter raised an eyebrow in confusion as she hurried toward the counter, pretending to be unpacking her work bag.

"Big meeting today?" he asked, his face now looking amused.

Now it was Paige who looked confused. *Is he actually speaking to me voluntarily?*

"What? Why are you—"

"I noticed this morning you were more dressed up."

Paige was caught between confusion and mild flattery.

"It's just," he continued, "you didn't seem in the mood for any compliments earlier, but you look nice today."

He said it so flippantly that she didn't know how to respond. And before she could get anything out, Carter grabbed a juice from the fridge and went to his room.

So, he's complimenting me now? This day could not get weirder.

She and Carter started the day in a staring standoff, then she was trapped on an elevator with Chance, and now Carter was handing out oddly phrased compliments to her. If her mind hadn't already been spinning, it definitely was now.

Paige figured it would be best to keep her brain busy, so she heated a frozen meal, worked for an hour on her business plan, and turned in for the night.

***

The next week and a half was more of the same. At home, Paige only saw Carter occasionally, which was fine with her. He hadn't made any more comments about the Christmas decor or about finding a new place to live. And while he was generally less rude, he hadn't offered any more semi-compliments either. They mostly acted as ships passing in the night, though Paige couldn't quite shake the image of Carter's smile, or the glimpse she had gotten of his abs the day he moved in. She hated to admit how much brain space she had given this man.

At work, Paige was doing everything she could to avoid any more run-ins with Chance or Diana, which had been a success with the continued help of Jenny and Laura.

The closest call had come when she was walking toward the break room to grab her lunch and spotted them on their way out. Luckily, they were deep in conversation that included puppy-dog eyes from both parties, so they didn't notice her pivot to take the long way around.

This last year was arguably one of the hardest years of Paige's life, and just when she had started feeling better, her best friend told her she was moving out, she lost her end-of-year bonus, she had to put up with an arrogant asshole of a roommate, and then learn that her cheating ex proposed to the woman he cheated on her with only a year before.

She was counting down the days until she left for Christmas with her family in California. In fact, it was one of the few things keeping her sane.

And now, only one more thing stood in the way of her enjoying a sunny and sixty-degree holiday with her family—her company's annual Christmas party.

Paige was dreading this day most of all. Not only did this mark the year anniversary of Chance admitting his affair, which was trauma-inducing enough, but it was yet another opportunity for him and Diana to flaunt their new engagement.

She didn't dare skip, as much as she wanted to. She didn't want to look weak for avoiding the event, and also Paige's boss was adamant that the entire team show up since they were inviting some of their top-tier clients this year. Not that any of these were *her* clients. It wasn't a battle she wanted to take on with her boss, who would, unfortunately, be her boss even longer now that she was bonus-less and soon-to-be roommate-less.

Paige's only choice was to dress to impress in an effort to show everyone she had moved on and was thriving. And thankfully, she had made some impulse purchases on Cyber Monday for some killer dresses.

Nadia arrived after work on Thursday with their usual wine and sushi to help her decide on her outfit for the Friday night party. It was their last hangout together before Paige left for California on Saturday, and before Nadia would likely be engaged.

Nadia and Linus traded years with their families at Christmas, and this year was their year to stay in Illinois. He had been dropping major hints that this holiday would be extra special, and Nadia confirmed it when she accidentally found the ring box while she cleared out some drawers for her stuff at his—or now, their—apartment.

"Should we place bets on how he will do it?" Nadia asked while they ate their sushi.

"Yes! Okay, my money is on ice skating at Millennium Park Ice Rink. How can you beat getting down on one knee by the massive Christmas tree and the Bean?" Paige said.

"That's definitely a strong contender," Nadia replied. "As cliché as it sounds, I think he will go with the ring in a champagne glass at The Walnut Room in Macy's. You know they have that massive tree up in the restaurant every year."

"Hmm, that is also a good one." Paige took a big sip of her wine. "As cool as he tries to come off, he really is a big cheeseball."

"Yes, and a romantic at heart." Nadia couldn't keep from smiling as she said it.

Paige really did love seeing her friend in love.

"All right, enough about me! Let's pick a dress that will make Chance do a double take," Nadia demanded as they finished their last bites of sushi.

Paige went to her closet and changed into a skin-tight black dress with sheer sleeves. She liked how she looked as she turned in front of the mirror, then went to show Nadia.

"Okay, this one is hot, but like, funeral hot," Nadia said. "Not sure it fits the Christmas party vibe you're going for."

"Fair enough." Paige went back to her closet and changed into the second option—a maroon-red midi dress with a high neck and pearl accents.

"I don't love you in this color, and this feels like what you'd wear to a country club event with people your parents are trying to impress," Nadia admitted.

"Yeah, I think you're right." Paige retreated to her closet for option three.

She put on a long velvet emerald-green dress with a low-cut neckline and high slit that showcased her toned leg.

These Pilates classes have really paid off, Paige thought to herself as she looked in the mirror before heading back out to Nadia.

"Umm, okay green goddess," Nadia chimed. "The green is a perfect match for your hair color, and it makes the green in your eyes pop!"

Paige felt hot in this dress, which was definitely the confidence boost she was going to need tomorrow when she walked into the party.

"So, it's settled then," Paige said. "Green light on the green."

A big gust of wind outside the window distracted the girls from their fashion show.

"Geez, I didn't think it was supposed to be snowing this much," Nadia groaned. "I think I should walk back home now. It looks like the snow is falling faster, and I'd rather get home before it's too bad. I hope it slows down soon so your party doesn't get cancelled. It would be a shame if the world didn't get to see you in this dress."

Paige snuck another peek at herself in the mirror and couldn't help but agree.

"Oh, I'm sure it will be fine."

"And you're sure you don't want me to tag along as your plus-one? I can tell Linus to cancel our dinner reservations."

Paige had debated bringing Nadia along with her for moral support, but ultimately decided it was something she needed to face on her own.

"Thanks, Nadia, but I'll be fine. Besides, my boss will expect us to be chatting with the clients, so I'll be occupied most of the time," Paige assured her as they walked toward the door. "Text me when you get back to your apartment so I know you made it! And you better call me immediately when you get engaged."

"Obviously." Nadia smiled and rolled her eyes. "I'll be dialing your number before I even say yes. Enjoy San Diego and give your mom and dad big hugs from me."

They shared a long and tight embrace before Nadia ventured out into the lugubrious scene. Paige could barely see Nadia through the flurry of snow as she made her way all bundled up down the sidewalk.

It really is coming down, isn't it, she thought. *The party getting cancelled wouldn't be the worst thing . . .*

She turned back toward the kitchen and screamed, "Oh my god!"

She hadn't heard Carter come out of his room.

"Sorry, I didn't mean to scare you," he said, not hiding the fact that he was scanning her from head to toe. Paige had forgotten she was still in the dress and could feel her face blushing.

Green is a nice color on you, she remembered him saying the morning after he saw her on her date. Clearly, he still felt the same way.

Carter ran his hand through his hair, looking slightly embarrassed that he had just undressed his landlord with his eyes.

"I, uh, found a new place to live," he said, breaking the awkward silence. "The contract starts January 4th, so unfortunately for both of us I'll be here until then."

His tone was both sarcastic and condescending at the same time. It took everything in Paige not to stab him in the eye with her used chopsticks before tossing them into the trash. But she decided to play it cool.

"Fine with me. I leave in two days anyway to go home for Christmas. Try not to suck up all the joy in here while I'm gone." She gave him a wink and a coy smile as she realized the dress really was giving her confidence.

His jaw muscles twitched, and Paige knew she had gotten under his skin. *See how he likes it.*

"Nice," Carter countered, seeming to struggle with his usual calm demeanor. He also seemed to be having a hard time keeping his eyes from straying back down to her V-neck dress.

"Don't you have any other words in your vocabulary?" Paige said in a mocking voice, mimicking Carter's insult from a couple of weeks earlier.

And then there it was again, the smile that could be the envy of any Hollywood actor, curling up one side of Carter's face.

"Wow, she jokes," he said sarcastically, holding eye contact with her before speaking again. "I'll send you money for the last half of December since I won't be leaving until January. Oh, and by the way, you don't need a plus-one in a dress like that."

Paige clocked his eyes stealing another quick scan of the dress, and she felt her face heating up.

Remember you hate him, she repeated over and over in her mind. Her brain knew this, but the butterflies in her stomach—and in more southern regions—weren't getting the memo.

Paige stared at him as he walked toward her. It was only then that she realized he had been holding a leftover container, and she was still standing by the trash can.

She was frozen in place as he stood next to her, sliding the cupboard that hid the trash bin out and disposing of what she could only assume was his dinner. His body gave off a wave of heat that Paige wanted to curl up in.

Damn it, he smells good.

She couldn't help but feel like Carter lingered for a second longer than he needed to before turning back toward his room. The magnetic feeling of standing close to him was something she hadn't felt in a long time, and she hated the rush it gave her.

Her phone buzzed, breaking her trance. A text from Nadia:

You know, if you really want to piss Chance off you could always ask Carter to be your plus-one ;)

She laughed and noticed Carter's head turn back toward her out of the corner of her eye. Paige retreated to her room to hang up the dress and felt his stare on her back until she shut the door.

Once she was back in her sweats, she threw her suitcase on her bed, still coming down from the high she had just felt standing next to Carter. As she started packing for a California Christmas, she fantasized about walking into the party arm in arm with Carter and seeing the looks on everyone's faces. Paige was so lost in thought she forgot about the snow falling outside her window.

Chapter 9

*H*ow *can Friday the 13th be both lucky and unlucky at the same time?* Paige thought as she looked at her phone.

She checked the weather app and saw snowflakes lighting up her screen. *Had it been snowing all night?* It didn't look like the snow would be slowing down anytime soon, but none of the news channels were predicting anything more than a couple of inches.

Her boss had sent out an email letting her team know they could work remotely for the day due to the weather, which she greatly appreciated. But the jury was still out on whether the Christmas party would be cancelled.

As much as Paige secretly hoped this would happen, it would mean not putting the dress back on and catching Carter looking in her direction. And Paige hated to admit she was looking forward to his attention.

On cue, Carter emerged from his room in workout attire. His only acknowledgement of her was a brief nod in her direction before rummaging through the fridge for his protein shake, which quickly reminded Paige that her fantasy about Carter returning a crush on her was just that—a fantasy.

She was looking forward to going home and seeing her parents. Even though Paige had re-decorated her condo after Carter's tirade, he had definitely sucked out some of the holiday spirit she had been craving after last year's breakup. Paige needed the Christmas coziness her parent's house provided ASAP.

Paige eyed the window nervously. Most of the flights out of Chicago were experiencing extreme delays today, and she hoped the tides would turn before her own flight tomorrow.

She pushed the thought out of her mind and opened up her laptop. Before jumping into work emails, she opened up her business plan budget.

Carter had sent over half of a month's rent last night to cover the remainder of his time in the condo. While it was still a nice bump to her savings, she needed to figure out where things stood with her freelance timeline.

After her last-minute shopping spree for a Christmas party outfit, her mortgage payment, and groceries for Thanksgiving, Paige had made only a small dent in what she hoped to save before making the leap and quitting her job. It was enough to cover a website domain and hosting platform and a subscription to her favorite graphic design software, which would allow her to get started on her branding while she waited to find a new roommate and beef up her savings. It wasn't anything major, but it was a step in the right direction.

She crunched some numbers and came to the conclusion that with the time it would take her to find a new roommate, and knowing they likely wouldn't be willing to pay the premium Carter had agreed to, it would be another six months before she felt comfortable leaving her job.

Paige sighed. *Maybe I was too harsh on Carter. Having him stay would have expedited the timeline.*

Sure, he was a grumpy, rude, arrogant ass, but she could have looked beyond all of that for the sake of his rent check. Paige was kicking herself for reacting with such a hot head after his Grinchy outburst.

Carter left his room again—this time in a white button-down with navy slacks. Paige couldn't help but do a double take as he made his way to the door and put on his jacket. Even with layers he was sexy.

He opened the door and left without a word or glance in her direction, and Paige reluctantly got started on work.

***

To Paige's relief, the party was cancelled. The company sent out an email just after lunch.

As hot as she felt in her party dress, she had some PTSD around the event that was starting to bubble up. She knew she wouldn't be able to avoid Chance and Diana forever, but the cancellation meant she could at least avoid them until after the holidays.

She'd take it.

Now, what to do on my last night in town?

Paige had planned her flight home around the mandatory Christmas party and was mostly packed for the trip, so now she had the night wide open.

She had used up the last of her groceries this week in preparation for her two-week trip, so she opened up the takeout app on her phone and searched through the available options.

The weather must be getting worse, she thought. *It seems like most restaurants are closed tonight.*

She put in an order at a fast-food chicken chain a few blocks away and opened up Instagram.

"All dressed up with nowhere to go!"

Of course it was Chance's post at the top of her feed again. The photo was of him and Diana in their Christmas party outfits standing in Chance's living room. She sighed and finally hit the unfollow button.

Any relief Paige had felt about the party getting cancelled quickly subsided. This post was just another reminder of last year's heartache and of what she no longer had.

She tried so hard to always be optimistic, but these past several weeks had started to test her limits on seeing the glass half full.

Four years ago she was polishing her resumé to get a better job, but then Chance walked into her life and sidetracked all of her plans. And for what? Sticking it out at the agency and making a crappy salary had felt worthwhile when she thought Chance was her soulmate. But now here she was feeling like she was totally behind in life.

As she looked out the window at the falling snow, she wished she had a partner to bundle up with for the walk to pick up her dinner—someone to snuggle up with on the couch under a cozy blanket.

She was a strong, independent woman who always looked for the bright side, but that didn't mean she couldn't use the company and partnership of a man.

Paige put on her puffy coat and gloves for her walk to the restaurant. She was about to open the front door when she heard an angry Carter on the other side.

"There is nothing more to discuss," he growled. "I'm done with this conversation."

Paige didn't have time to move away from the door before he opened it, catching her like a deer in the headlights.

The look on Carter's face warned of his sour mood.

"Move," he practically grunted.

Paige knew he had caught her eavesdropping, but his command made her blood boil.

"What's got your panties in a bunch?" She knew she was pushing dangerous buttons, but if he was going to be rude, she wasn't going to just lay down and take it. Besides, at this point she had been wallowing in self-pity for the past half hour and had no shits left to give.

"Not in the mood," he said coolly as he slid past her.

"So I take it you don't want to walk with me and talk about it?" she said sarcastically, pushing harder.

Carter turned on his heels to glare at her. His brown eyes almost looked like they were on fire. Then the corner of his mouth twitched up in a smile, like he enjoyed her testing his boundaries.

"Not in the slightest," he said before turning back around and closing himself in his bedroom.

"Asshole," Paige muttered under breath as she started her trek to get dinner.

***

Later that night as Paige was brushing her teeth, she couldn't shake her annoyance at her interaction with Carter earlier. This man really had the gall to check her out one day and then the next, treat her like she was trash on the sidewalk he could kick out of his way.

Just hours earlier she was regretting kicking him out, but now Paige was counting down the hours until her plane was set to take off and bring her far away from this disrespectful and inconsiderate jerk.

She had been checking the news and flight app all evening to make sure everything was still on track. The meteorologist seemed to take a casual stance on the snow falling outside, which eased Paige's mind as she got into bed and drifted to sleep.

***

The following morning shocked the entire city of Chicago.

While everyone slept, the city experienced the biggest blizzard it had seen since 1979.

There was twenty-nine inches of snow on the ground and it showed no signs of stopping. And on top of that, it was fifteen degrees outside.

O'Hare and Midway were both completely shut down, and there was no world in which Paige was getting on a plane to California.

How did this happen? Paige was shocked. *Why did none of the news channels pick up on this storm?*

She looked out her window onto a sea of white. Cars were covered, doors were blocked, and there wasn't a soul in sight.

She was completely snowed in.

It was only then that it dawned on her.

She wasn't snowed in.

They were snowed in.

Chapter 10

P aige was spiraling. Her flight was cancelled, and though she was already rebooked for the next day, she had little faith the snow was going anywhere that soon.

Her phone buzzed with a text from Nadia.

> Paige OMG! I'm so sorry about your flight . . . I know how much you were looking forward to going home.

> This storm came out of nowhere! What the hell?!

> I knowwwww. It's so wild!

Can I come over to your place if I can shovel my way out of the condo building?

Obviously you are always welcome, BUT when we realized the snow was coming down hard last night we preemptively drove out to Linus's parents' house :/

Well then it's official . . . I'm stuck in here with Carter.

I mean . . . there could be worse things ;)

Nadia, there is NOTHING worse! He is insufferable. Just when I thought we were turning a corner, he comes in hot with his holier than thou attitude that reminds me why I hate him.

I'm sorry, I wish I could do something!

Paige set her phone down and made a coffee.

As she waited for the cup to fill up, she counted the remaining pods for her Nespresso machine. 1, 2, 3, 4, 5, 6 . . .

"What are you still doing here?"

Paige startled at the sound of Carter's voice. "You don't know?" Paige asked as she turned around to see a shirt-less, god-like Carter standing in the doorway.

It was a good thing her coffee wasn't ready, or she would have dropped the mug.

His olive skin was so smooth, he looked like stone. The muscles helped with that too. His triceps were bulging, as if he had just done 100 push-ups before opening the door. His chest was muscular and led down to a six-pack chiseled to perfection.

She had no idea how much time had passed when she heard Carter speak again. "Holy shh . . ." His voice trailed off as he walked to the window.

While she was in her trance, he must have grabbed a shirt because he was pulling one on as he passed her.

Had he noticed her staring? *Great*, she thought. *How long was I gaping at him?*

"This is bad," Carter said. "Very bad."

"No shit, Sherlock," Paige replied. "At this point, we are completely snowed in."

"So, no flight for you then." He was still looking out the window.

"Again, your detective skills are unparalleled," Paige said.

Carter turned toward her, jaw muscles clenched. She was getting under his skin again.

He began walking across the room to where she stood, but he walked right past her to the coffee machine.

"Ahh thanks, roomie. I was really craving a good cup of joe this morning." Carter picked up the mug and took a sip, maintaining eye contact the whole time.

Paige couldn't believe he had the nerve but was finding it hard to summon words as she looked into his eyes.

She had never seen them this close in the daylight before. They were such a light shade of brown they almost looked yellow.

"If you'd like to take a picture, it'll last longer." Carter leaned back against the counter with a smile.

"Oh, don't flatter yourself," Paige said, snapping out of her second trance of the morning. "I'm just trying to understand where you get off being such a prick. Move," she barked at him, and she stepped to the coffee machine, nudging him firmly with her shoulder.

See how he likes being ordered around.

"Geez, can't a guy have his coffee in peace?" he said after regaining his balance.

Paige didn't humor him with a reply.

As she made herself another coffee, Carter spoke again, "Look, I don't like this either. I'd much rather go out to the gym, the coffee shop, the grocery store—heck, I'd even rather go into work than be stuck inside an apartment where it looks like a Christmas bomb went off. But here we are."

"Why do you hate Christmas so much, anyway?"

Carter looked down into his now half-empty mug, his face taking on the solemn look she had seen a couple of times before. "I just think it's overhyped is all," he said with a small shrug. He proceeded to take another sip of coffee.

Paige wasn't sure she was buying it. Could he really have *that* bad of an attitude because he felt the holiday was overhyped? But she was still annoyed that he had stolen her first coffee so she didn't press any further. As she walked toward the couch to turn on the news, she simply said, "If you say so."

She heard the door to his room close shortly after, followed by the news anchor's advice for everyone to stay indoors until the blizzard subsided.

With that, she wrapped herself up in her favorite blanket, hit play on a cheesy Christmas movie, and soon after closed her eyes for a nap.

***

A couple of hours later, Paige was startled awake by the sound of rummaging in the refrigerator.

"Can't you see I'm napping here?" she groaned. As she said it, her stomach did the same.

"What the hell are we going to eat?" Carter said, ignoring her.

Shit. Paige hadn't thought that far ahead. This morning she had been so worried about coffee and being snowed in with her Christmas nemesis that she hadn't even thought about meals—and she had used up the last of her groceries the day before.

Paige got up and walked over to the fridge. She and Carter stood side by side looking at nearly bare shelves, save for a bag of shredded cheese, butter, condiments, and a carton of a dozen eggs.

Carter pulled out the freezer drawer, and the prospects weren't much better. One frozen pizza, a bag of breakfast sausages, two half-empty tubs of ice cream, and a bag of veggies.

The pantry cupboard had pancake mix, syrup, pasta noodles and sauce, an already opened bag of tortilla chips, and most everything needed for baking.

Paige took stock of the options and figured they had about three meals at best.

"Okay, so there's pizza for one meal, pancakes and omelets with sausage for another, and spaghetti and tortilla chips. Plus, looks like I can make chocolate chip cookies to hold us over in between," Paige said.

"I have some protein bars stashed in my room," Carter chimed in. "I'll throw them in the cupboard as another backup."

Without giving it a second thought, Paige grabbed Carter's bicep and squeezed. "You might want to eat one now. Your arm seems a bit weak," she said. She wasn't sure why she had done it—perhaps she was still groggy from her nap—but Carter's muscle was rock solid and she had to force her hand back to her own pocket.

"Sorry." She blushed. "That was so weird."

She debated glancing back at his face, nervous that he would look appalled, but she took the risk. And there it was—her favorite smile had returned, curling up more on the right side and showcasing some of his picture-perfect teeth.

"Living here has been nothing short of interesting," Carter said. "Any more fitness tips?" As the words came out of his mouth, he purposefully lifted his arms to the back of his head, displaying his biceps and lifting his shirt just enough to show off his lower abdominals.

Stop looking, Paige, she thought. *He is a coffee-stealing, self-centered asshole, remember?*

"Sorry, the first tip is complimentary. After that, I charge in caffeine, compliments, or cold hard cash." Her quick reply struck a chord with Carter because he let out the type of laugh that comes from deep within. She had never heard him laugh before, but it was contagious enough to put a smile on her face.

"Okay," Paige continued, "let's get serious so we don't wither away in here . . . which meal do we make first?"

She opened up the refrigerator again to stare at the items. Carter stood behind her, and Paige could feel the warmth of his body at her back, contrasting the cool air coming from the fridge. Her heartbeat was racing, and she hoped he wasn't able to hear the pounding in her chest.

It wasn't until he pushed off the open doors that she realized she had been holding her breath.

"You choose," he called over his shoulder nonchalantly, disappearing into his bedroom.

Chapter 11

She landed on pizza.

It was the easiest option, so she set the oven, sat down at the kitchen island, and checked the news.

It wasn't looking good.

The snow wasn't letting up, and there were photos sent in from all around the city with frozen car doors, icicles, and almost three feet of snow everywhere. The snowplows were having a hard time getting around, and what was the point when the snow kept falling? It was getting too risky for them to be out there.

There was a time in her life when the only thing she'd asked Santa for was snow. *I guess Santa saved up all my childhood wishes for this moment.*

She definitely wasn't going to San Diego anytime soon. And with the state of things, it didn't seem like she'd be going anywhere. No restaurants were open, and it seemed very few grocery stores were open. For now, she'd have to make whatever random items she had in the kitchen last.

She popped the pizza in the oven and opened up Instagram. All she saw in her feed was snow, as if the blizzard was taunting her. It seemed everyone in Chicago wanted to make sure the world remembered what three feet of snow looked like.

Without thinking, she started typing Chance's name in the search bar. She wasn't sure why she was torturing herself, but she chalked it up to the fact that it was exactly a year ago he admitted to sleeping with Diana.

She clicked on his story and saw the pair in matching Santa hats and ugly Christmas sweaters, cheersing mugs of hot chocolate. As much as Paige was over Chance, she'd always loved how much he got into the holiday spirit. He had always matched her and her family's enthusiasm for Christmas, something she really missed, especially considering Carter's attitude about it all.

As if on cue, she heard his voice behind her. "That is the stupidest thing I've ever seen."

Startled, Paige quickly locked her phone before saying, "Has no one ever told you it's rude to snoop?"

"Who's in the photo?"

"What?" she replied.

"You were staring at that picture for a long time," Carter said. "So, who's in it?"

"Well, I'm not surprised you don't recognize Santa when you see him, given you are the literal Grinch." Paige hoped Carter would take the bait and drop it.

"Haha. You know avoiding the answer is only making this more interesting. Who is it?" he pressed, narrowing his eyes at her.

"Not that it is any of your business, but it's my ex and his new girlfr—uh, fiancée."

Carter opened his mouth to speak again just as the pizza timer went off.

"Well, look at that," Paige said. "That's all the time we had for questions. Thanks for participating."

She got up and took the pizza out of the oven, found the pizza cutter, and grabbed plates, willing herself to look busy so Carter wouldn't ask any follow-up questions.

And he didn't.

She wasn't sure if the sting in her chest was from thinking about Chance and their breakup anniversary, or from Carter not caring to know more. After their banter earlier, she was finally feeling like maybe—just maybe—his icy exterior was just a front.

She slid a plate with two pizza slices over to him.

"Thanks," Carter said with a soft smile. "Oh, and also, thanks for sharing your food with me. I never cook—pretty much only rely on takeout—so this blizzard really bit me in the ass."

"Don't mention it. I always meant to treat you to a frozen pizza, remember?" Paige nudged his shoulder as she took the seat next to him at the island. He was almost done with his first piece.

They sat in silence for a minute before she continued, "I mean, I know you have barely touched the kitchen here, but you seriously *never* cook?"

"Never," Carter said, finishing off his second slice. "There's one thing I know how to make and that's it. Otherwise, I've just always had someone else cooking for me, whether it was my mom, restaurants . . . friends."

Paige noticed the pause before the last word. She almost thought it was like he was trying to decide what he wanted to say. The thought of him being fresh out of a breakup popped back into her mind, but she brushed it off. *I just mentioned my ex, I'm sure he would mention his too.*

"Well, that is just sad. Cooking and baking can be so therapeutic and fun." Paige elbowed him playfully. "I did a lot of baking after my breakup. It helped me think and process."

"Eh, I don't feel like I'm missing much," Carter replied with a sarcastic smile.

"Well, that settles it then," Paige blurted out. "We're baking cookies."

"Finally a Christmas activity I can fully support," he teased.

Paige finished her last slice in a couple more bites and immediately got to work getting the leftover pizza in the fridge, putting the dirty dishes in the dishwasher, and gathering up all the ingredients for cookies. Thankfully, the oven was already preheated from the pizza.

Carter stood around the island awkwardly. *Man, he really never spends time in a kitchen*, Paige thought to herself.

After a minute, he started wiping some crumbs into his hand. Paige couldn't help but smile at his attempt to help clean up.

"So," she started, "what is the one meal you make?"

He hesitated. "You need to promise not to make fun of me for this."

"You have my word," she said mockingly, holding her hands to her heart.

"Pancakes." His tone was completely serious.

"Pancakes? Twisty. Why pancakes?"

"Well," he started, "that's the only thing my dad taught me to make. To be fair, it was the only thing *he* knew how to make. But when I say they are the best pancakes . . ." His voice trailed off.

Was. Past tense.

"Okay, so what makes these pancakes so special?" she asked, genuinely curious about how pancakes could possibly differ that much from one batch to another.

"It's all in the little things," he said. He looked like he was drifting off into a memory. "Sure, there are some unique ingredients, but it's about the order you put them in the bowl, how fast you whisk them together, when you flip the pancake. Most people don't give these a second thought, but they matter."

She had to try to keep her composure. If this sensitive guy standing across from her was the Carter that had showed up to the roommate interview that day, or the Carter that had moved into her condo a few weeks ago, she would surely have fallen head over heels by now.

"That's actually pretty interesting," she said. "Your dad . . . *was* a smart guy?" She turned the statement into a question in an effort to learn more about Carter's past.

"Yeah, he was. He died five years ago," Carter said, confirming her suspicions. "Car accident."

"I'm sorry, Carter. Were you guys close?"

"Yeah, yeah, we were. But it's all good." He shrugged, but she could still see some pain lingering in his eyes.

"Oh, by the way," he said, seeming to want to move on from the topic. "I'm sorry about your flight getting cancelled. I'm sure you were looking forward to going home."

Again with the sensitivity. This version of Carter may very well end me.

"Thanks. I'm bummed to miss time with my family, but at least the snow got me out of the company Christmas party," she confessed.

"Yeah, but it's a shame that dress didn't get its time to shine." Carter ran his hand through his hair and avoided eye contact with her.

Paige blushed and let out a giggle. "Actually, you're right. That is the one loss from it all. I was looking forward to seeing my ex's reaction to that little number."

Carter furrowed his brow in confusion. "Wait, I thought you said this was a company party? Do you *work* with your ex?"

"Yup. Well, I mean, we both work at the same company, in different departments, thank goodness. We met there."

"I see." Carter said, processing this information.

"He was going to be there with his new fiancée, who—get this—he cheated on me with. She was a new hire at our company. He confessed to sleeping with her at last year's Christmas party. And they just got engaged on Thanksgiving, so I've been on the receiving end of looks of pity for weeks."

Carter was momentarily speechless, staring at Paige with a look of awe.

"Let me get this straight—you were going to show up at this party in front of your idiot ex and petty colleagues all by yourself? In *that* dress?"

Paige wasn't sure if he thought she was insane or badass, but when he let out a laugh and shook his head, it confirmed he was at least a little bit impressed. She felt her face heating up and quickly changed the subject.

"When was the last time you made them?" she asked. "The pancakes."

"Hmm, probably like three years ago now. Back when I was trying to woo my last girlfriend," he said with a wink.

"Ahh, I see. The perfect trick for getting girls into bed. Make them pancakes," Paige said with a smile.

"Well, technically it was my move to get them *back* into bed with me," Carter confessed. "I'd get up in the morning, feed a girl my famous pancakes, and it usually charmed them enough for . . . seconds."

"Men are so gross." Paige rolled her eyes.

He gave a casual shrug. Paige's mind turned back to Carter's original answer to her question. He had said it was three years since he had made them, and then the words *"last girlfriend."* Was he recently single, or did he just happen to grow out of his playboy phase? She wanted to know the answer but didn't want to scare him off while they were actually having a good conversation.

"Okay, so . . . cookies?" she asked, breaking from her thoughts. "You can help me measure out what we need while I get everything mixed together."

He got up from the chair and made his way around the island. As he reached for the measuring cups, his hand brushed her arm, and just like the other night by the trash can, she felt something like electricity pass between them.

Did he feel it too? She wondered. They spent the next few minutes mostly in silence while they worked in tandem, reading off the go-to chocolate chip cookie recipe Paige kept on her phone.

"Okay, so what next?" asked Carter when he was done measuring.

"Now I combine everything together," she said. "And then add some secret ingredients."

"Oh, now we're talking," he said eagerly. "Am I allowed to know?"

"Well, we need to make this snow day exciting, don't we?" She gave him a coy smile. "First secret . . . I put in a few dashes of cinnamon." She shook the spice into the mixing bowl.

"And then," she continued, "pass me the salt."

Carter reached over and grabbed the pink retro Santa saltshaker. "Is this really necessary?"

"What?" Paige asked. "Is it really so bad to like Christmas?"

Carter smiled and let out a small laugh as he handed her the Santa shaker. "No, I suppose it's not."

Paige added the salt to the bowl, did her final mix, and started scooping the batter onto the baking tray. "Here," she said, handing him a spoon. "You can start filling up this tray."

They stood side by side arranging their cookie dough. Paige occasionally noticed Carter sneaking a peek at her tray, likely making sure he was doing it right.

As he filled the last spot on his tray, his phone lit up from where it was lying across the island.

Mom.

He quickly wiped his hands on a towel and danced around the counter to grab it before it stopped ringing.

"Hey, Ma," he answered, breathing heavily from the quick movement. "Yeah, yeah, I'm all good, but it's really coming down out there . . . Yeah, you can barely see out the window. But we've got some things here for meals, so don't worry . . ."

Paige could barely make out a *"Who is we?"* on the other side of the line.

"My roommate, Ma," said Carter. "Yes, she was kind enough to share some frozen pizza and now she is baking cookies . . . Yes, she *is* being too nice to me." He winked across the room at her.

Was he winking because he said the word nice—their one inside joke—or because he was being flirty? Paige secretly hoped it was the latter. She shot him a shy smile before turning to put the cookies in the oven.

"I know," Carter continued. "I already have a reminder set to call Gram. I do put birthdays in my calendar, you know . . . Yes, I will keep you updated on the blizzard. Don't worry, there are more than enough Christmas blankets in here to keep us warm." He smiled as he made his way toward his room. "I know you're concerned, Ma, but I promise I'll be fine . . ."

He was still smiling as he closed the door to his room.

So this is what his icy exterior has been hiding this whole time, Paige thought. Carter came off as a real jerk, but seeing this side of him today changed everything she thought she knew about her roommate.

Just this morning, he had stolen her freshly made cup of coffee, but the guy she had spent the last hour with was a completely different person. He was thoughtful, open, and vulnerable.

Sure, he looked like a walking Abercrombie model, but apparently he was also a man who called his grandmother on her birthday without needing to be reminded—and that elevated his attractiveness even more than Paige could have imagined.

Paige hadn't had feelings like this in a long time. The butterflies in her stomach wouldn't stop fluttering. She so badly wanted what Nadia and Linus had—what she thought she had with Chance—but she was too afraid of opening herself up for heartbreak again to ever give anyone new a chance.

She always found some excuse for not dating. Too soon. Too busy. Too expensive. After all, Chicago wasn't cheap, and she wasn't the type to insist that a guy always has to pay.

The day had been full of surprises, perhaps the most surprising thing being her realization that she might be ready to actually start dating for real again. But was she ready to date in general, or ready to date Carter? She didn't even know if he was interested in her like that. And besides, he was her roommate. At least for now.

Paige put on some Christmas music and started washing all the dishes while the cookies continued to bake.

Carter emerged from his room twenty minutes later just as she was taking them out of the oven.

"Perfect timing," he said as he slid onto an island stool. "They smell incredible."

He reached for the tray and Paige swatted his hand away.

"Not so fast," she said. "There is one final touch."

She sprinkled some sea salt onto the soft tops of the cookies.

"There, now they're done." She handed him the one that looked the best.

Carter took a bite into the gooey center and gave a nod of satisfaction while he chewed.

"Paige," he started, mouth still full of cookie. God, she loved hearing him say her name, even like this. "This is the best cookie I've ever had," he said. "I'm honored to have learned from the master."

What a dork.

"The pleasure was all mine," she said with a smile. "I'm just glad we . . ." She hesitated before her next words. Was it too forward to tell him she enjoyed spending the afternoon with him? Man, she was so out of practice when it came to this stuff. "I'm just glad we didn't burn them." She decided to take the safe route. "Seeing as we don't have much extra food to spare."

She stole a glance at Carter and could have sworn there was a slight look of disappointment on his face before he looked over to her and said, "Same here. I'm *very* glad we didn't burn them."

He maintained eye contact as he reached over the counter again to grab two more cookies. He took a couple of steps out of the kitchen and stopped, but instead of turning around and rejoining her in the kitchen, he kept walking straight into his room and closed the door.

Paige felt a twinge of disappointment that Carter didn't stick around. She couldn't believe how easy it was to hang out with him now that he had let his walls down.

Why do I feel like I miss talking to him already? Paige thought to herself. *This is crazy, right?*

She replayed the last few minutes over and over in her head while she moved all the cookies into plastic containers and cleaned the last of the day's dishes.

I should have just told him I was enjoying hanging out with him. It's not like it was that forward. Plus, I don't think I'm imagining the look that was on his face. He genuinely seemed hurt that I wasn't glad to spend time with him. When he comes back out again I think I'm going to tell him.

She made a hot chocolate and took her usual position on the couch and put on one of the Netflix Christmas movies she hadn't gotten around to yet, keeping her peripheral vision on Carter's room in case he came back out.

***

Paige was already halfway through a second movie when the door to Carter's room opened. She paused and turned toward the kitchen.

"Hey, Car—" she started before quickly noticing the over-the-ear headphones he was wearing, his music loud enough even she could hear it. He kept his back to her as he pulled out leftover pizza slices from the refrigerator, and then he didn't look her way as he took them—still cold—back to his room.

And just like that, she thought, *the old Carter is back.*

Paige rolled her eyes and resumed the movie, willing herself to ignore the ache building up in her chest.

Chapter 12

T he city looked the same the next morning. There was still at least three feet of powder on the ground, with snow continuing to flurry. It was hard for Paige to see down the street from her bedroom window.

She checked the airline app and saw exactly what she expected—*CANCELLED*.

Looks like I have another day locked up with him.

She slept terribly. As much as she hated to admit it to herself, she had developed a big crush on Carter. Sure, she thought he was handsome from the day she laid eyes on him in Starbucks, but there was something about their interactions yesterday that had her heart in a full-on tailspin. And Carter blatantly ignoring her at the end of the night not only hurt, but it re-solidified her initial reasons for hating him.

> Hmm, that sounds so strange! And you're SURE there was no little wave or smile?

Nadia's text read.

Paige had texted Nadia the full synopsis of her day before she had gone to bed.

> I'm positive. It was like the time we spent actually hanging out never even happened. I'm almost starting to wonder if I dreamt it all?

> I'm sure there is a reason. I know he hasn't been the warmest roommate, but I just can't believe he was purposely icing you out.

> Nadia, why are you constantly Team Carter? You are ALWAYS defending him.

> I'm not team Carter, Paige. I'm just trying to give him the benefit of the doubt, that's all. Based on what you told me about yesterday, it sounds like there's a really good guy in there. Don't write him off just yet.

Paige heard some rattling coming from the kitchen.

> Well, I think I hear him in the kitchen. I guess I'll just go out there and see what his reaction is. But if he ignores me again, I swear I'm gonna kick him out in the cold . . .

Haha, well, I have a good feeling you'll be
snuggling together for warmth soon ;)

Paige grabbed the Christmas sweater that was lying on
the chair in her room, pulled it on over her T-shirt, and
opened her bedroom door to the smell of pancakes and
coffee.

"Morning, roomie," Carter said with a smile. "I thought
I heard your water running so I figured I'd get started on
breakfast . . . well,"—he looked at the clock—"brunch."

Paige immediately noticed that his black T-shirt had
dust from the pancake mix on the front, which somehow
made him look even hotter. He flicked his head to get
a runaway strand of his hair away from his eyes as he
flipped over the pancake he had on the pan. It was the
perfect golden color.

She was too shocked to say anything.

"I hope it's okay I'm using the kitchen and all of your
pans," he said, filling the silence. "I just got a bit too
excited to show off my one culinary ability. Oh! And
there's a coffee for you." He pointed at the Nespresso
machine.

Sure enough, there was a coffee that still had steam
coming off the top waiting for her. *Who is this man, and
what has he done with the Carter I saw last night?*

"No, no, of course it's fine! Sorry, I'm just surprised, that's all," Paige said, grabbing the mug.

"All right, one pancake ready to go." Carter handed her a plate with a perfectly cooked pancake on it. She sat down at the island, where he had already laid out silverware and syrup.

"What's the occasion?" She asked him, still in disbelief that she was receiving royal treatment.

"Well, for starters, a thank-you for sharing your rations with me. Next, because it felt aligned with the Christmas spirit you're so *desperately* trying to summon in here," he teased. "But also, I was just looking for an excuse to try to impress a girl."

His back was turned because he was mid-pancake flip, which Paige was grateful for. Her cheeks were warm from blushing, and she didn't want to give Carter the satisfaction of knowing his little trick was working on her.

After all, *this was his move,* she had to remind herself. *He does this for his own purposes—don't fall into the trap.*

She composed herself just as he was turning to give her a second pancake. Perfect, again.

"Well, it takes a lot to impress me," she quipped. She put the first bite in her mouth.

Carter stood across the counter wide-eyed, waiting eagerly for her review.

"I'll hand it to you," she said after savoring and swallowing the bite, "this is a near-perfect pancake."

He smiled at her as if she had just told him he had won a million dollars.

"You hear that, Dad?" he said, looking up toward the ceiling. "Another fan of your work."

Paige's heart melted into a puddle to match the syrup on her plate. How could she stay mad at this guy? Before she could think it through, she blurted out, "So, what was up with you last night?"

"What do you mean?" he asked, looking suddenly confused.

"You completely ignored me when you came into the kitchen for that pizza. I started talking to you and—"

"Oh shit," he interrupted. "I'm really sorry. I was doing some exercises and was totally in the zone. I didn't hear you over my music. Seriously, I'm sorry." He paused before adding, "Now these are also apology pancakes."

Dammit, Nadia, Paige thought. *Of course he has a valid excuse.*

"Don't worry about it. Sorry I took it so personally. I just . . ." She hesitated again but decided to just come out with it. "I just wanted to say that, while yesterday started rough, not being able to go home and all, I ended up having a really fun day . . . with you."

A smile crept back across Carter's face.

"Me too," he said. "So I guess that means we really need to knock today out of the park now."

"I guess so," she agreed. "And if these pancakes are any indication, we are off to a great start." She stuffed another full bite into her mouth.

"There's more where that came from." Carter turned back to the stove and poured more batter onto the pan.

They spent their meal engaged in the usual small talk you make with someone you just met. Paige was surprised at how little she actually knew about the guy living in the room across the condo, and how little he knew about her.

Carter was in finance, which she had known, but she learned more about what his job entailed on a day-to-day basis and the direction he wanted to take his career. He talked more about his mom, and they bonded over growing up as only children. He talked about where he went to college—Duke—and she learned he was a student athlete on their lacrosse team.

That explains the body, Paige thought.

She told him about growing up in California and life on the west side of the country. She talked about her job at the marketing agency and how ready she was to leave. She even told him about her dream of freelance consulting.

"I think that sounds awesome," Carter said. "You should totally just go for it. Life is too short to continue doing something that makes you unhappy. It took me way too long to learn that."

"You know from experience?"

"Yeah, uh . . ." He paused briefly. "I guess you could say that, but I won't bore you with the details."

He stuffed a big bite of pancake into his mouth, leading to their first string of silence of the morning, but it gave Paige some time to clean up the dishes while she thought of what to say next. Talking with Carter was easy, and she wasn't ready for him to retreat to his room just yet.

"So, I'm thinking first on our list of activities for the day," Carter cut in before she could think of anything, "we compete in a friendly game of Mario Kart," he said as he pointed at the Nintendo Switch by the TV.

List of activities? Seems like I'm not the only one who wants more time together . . .

"Oh, heck yeah." Paige turned toward him. "Are you *sure* you're ready to get your ass handed to you so soon?"

Carter looked stunned at her reply.

"I see how it is. You don't know the can of worms you've just opened up." Carter smirked. His golden-brown eyes twinkled at the mention of competition.

"Bring it on," Paige said, throwing the dish towel on the counter and scurrying toward the TV.

The light trash talk only strengthened the tension that was building in the room.

They picked their characters—Princess Peach for Paige and Yoshi for Carter—and played for two hours straight, going tit for tat until their fingers were stiff. To spare their hands from permanent carpal tunnel, Carter proclaimed the next race was for all the marbles.

"What do you say we make this interesting?" he asked, narrowing his eyes at her.

Paige felt her cheeks starting to flush as she responded, "Keep talking . . . what do you have in mind?"

What the hell is he about to suggest? She thought. *And why do I low-key hope it's a game of strip Mario Kart?* She tried to shake the image of a shirtless Carter from her mind with little success.

"If I win," he said, "you put away ten Christmas decorations of my choosing, which will most definitely include that large Santa over there." He pointed at the corner across from his bedroom door where Paige and Nadia always put their vintage light-up Santa. It was technically meant to be an outdoor decoration, but the girls loved the classic Christmas vibe it brought to the condo.

"Oh, you mean the one that scares the shit out of you?" she teased.

Paige had noticed Carter jump on more than one occasion upon leaving his room, and although it was funny to see him get scared by a plastic decoration, she had to admit it *was* a bit much.

"I will neither confirm nor deny the answer to that question," he said, avoiding eye contact.

"Whatever you say, scaredy cat. So, what happens when I win?"

"*If* you win . . ." He paused while he contemplated his next words. "If you win, I will watch a Christmas movie of your choice with you tonight."

A little disappointing this isn't strip Mario Kart with his six-pack abs on display, but this is major progress.

"Wow, so you're telling me that if I win, Mr. Grinch himself will watch a full-length Christmas movie?"

"Yep. And if I win, then Mrs. Claus needs to send the tacky Santa back to storage. So, do we have a deal?" He stretched out his hand toward her. Despite his dig at her festive knickknacks, Paige shook it and felt that familiar electricity run through her as their skin touched.

They zoned in as the race started, mashing buttons and cursing at every inconvenience. On lap three, they were neck and neck until Paige got hit by a red shell from a computer player behind her, allowing Carter to take the lead. As she hit the gas again, a blue shell flew past her, its sights set on Carter.

The shell hit him just short of the finish line, taking out the computer opponent in its wake, allowing Paige to speed past them and over the finish line in first place.

Carter slung some expletives at the screen while Paige jumped up and down, pretending to bow for an invisible cheering crowd.

"Oh, Carter, don't look so . . . *shell*-shocked," she teased.

He stared at her blankly for a second before bursting into uncontrollable laughter. It was contagious enough that Paige joined in.

"Damn. You're pretty, funny, a cookie master, and you can whoop ass in Mario Kart. Why am I moving out?"

Paige's heart skipped a beat.

"Pretty, huh?" she asked, feeling bold.

Now it was Carter's turn to blush. She saw a slight pink tone appear in his olive skin.

"I'm quite sure I said *pretty funny*." He held her gaze, resisting a smile.

"My mistake then." She said, fully aware that she was now the one blushing as they maintained eye contact.

This has to be flirting, right? She thought. *Should I really be doing this? He is technically my tenant. And he seems like the kind of guy who flirts with any girl. Don't let him lure you into his charming trap, Paige. You don't want to get hurt again.*

"So," she said, snapping out of the trance. "What movie to pick?" She stroked her chin in thought.

"I'm at your mercy, oh Mario Kart champion." Carter bowed his head.

For being Chicago's hottest man, he sure is dorky, she noted. *Like I needed another reason to be more attracted to him. Focus, Paige, and* not *on Carter.*

"I'll give it some thought this afternoon. There's a lot riding on this decision, after all. This might be my only chance to show you the light," she said.

"No pressure." He grinned before adding, "All right then, I'm gonna go do a workout to get all this Mario Kart adrenaline out of my system." He jumped up from where he was sitting on the couch and made his way into his room.

Paige tidied up the kitchen and then the living room. A few minutes later, Carter's door opened. He was once again without a shirt. His skin was slightly dewy with sweat and his biceps were bulging.

Paige gawked at him as he walked over to the sink, water bottle in hand.

Thankfully, she regained her composure before he turned around and noticed her. He removed his headphones from one ear and said, "Forgot my water."

He gave her a slight head nod and proceeded back to his room again. Paige was still frozen in place, trying to process the image she had just seen.

If she hadn't already come to the conclusion, she was sure of it now—she was down bad for Carter.

In the past few weeks, she had decided she was open to dating again, but now . . . now she was realizing she might only be open to dating *Carter*. It would be impossible to get him out of her head now.

Even when he was being an asshole, he was in the back of her mind, and now that she was getting to know the man he actually was inside—and the man he was under his T-shirt—she couldn't shake the massive crush building up inside.

Paige could have sworn that he had been sending her flirty vibes. He said he made her pancakes to try to impress her, he had smiled when she told him she enjoyed their day together, he laughed at her jokes, and he definitely called her pretty—even though he tried to deny it.

But she just couldn't determine if any of this was genuine, or if it was all just a game he played to get women into bed.

I mean, come on, she thought. *A guy who looks like that can't possibly be flirting with me because he genuinely likes me.*

Paige was objectively attractive, and she wasn't a stranger to being on the receiving end of male attention, but Carter was just in a whole different league.

She didn't want to place any hope in him liking her back in *that* way. It would hurt too much if the feelings weren't reciprocated.

Plus, the jury was still out on whether he was recently single, and she didn't want to just be his rebound fling. She was already in too deep.

She finished folding a blanket and placed it over the back of the couch. Then she retreated to her room to call her parents in lieu of being on a plane to see them, and, most importantly, come up with the Christmas movie she would watch with Carter.

If they only had a few days together before she went home for Christmas—and before he moved out—she was determined to make the most of it.

Chapter 13

"I've made my decision," Paige announced later as she and Carter stood in the kitchen boiling spaghetti noodles. "We're watching *Elf*."

Paige didn't want to admit how much thought she'd put into this decision. It was borderline embarrassing.

She wanted to pick a movie that had some comedy, because she had picked up on the fact that Carter liked to laugh. And admittedly, *she* liked to watch *him* laugh. But it also had to have just the right amount of Christmas cheer without being too cheesy. The situation was delicate indeed. The wrong choice could cement Carter's dislike of Christmas, yes, but it could also paint her as just some girl who gets swept away in the Christmas fantasy.

Home Alone could be seen as too childish. *The Grinch* was too obvious. So, after careful consideration, *Elf* was the strongest contender.

"Oh, is that the one with the guy from *Step Brothers*?" Carter asked. "Will Ferrell, right?"

"Yep! Wait, have you seen this one?"

Don't tell me all my deliberation was for nothing.

Carter looked at her as if she had just asked the dumbest question in the world.

"I'll take that as a no," she said, answering her own question.

"I may not be a big Christmas fan, but I don't live under a rock. Every guy knows Will Ferrell's movies." He smiled.

They made some more small talk while the pasta finished cooking. Apparently, Carter had grown up on Nintendo games, which made his loss that afternoon even more painful. Every summer he'd spend his morning at a sports camp, and then all of his teammates would come over to play Super Smash Bros. and Mario Party.

Another point in the dorky column. She swooned silently.

Once the spaghetti was ready, they each made a bowl and headed toward the couch. Paige made sure to grab the plate of leftover cookies on her way.

She sat on the left corner of the couch and watched anxiously as Carter plopped down on the right corner. They couldn't be sitting farther apart if they wanted to. Paige had slightly hoped Carter would have pulled a bold move and sat down right next to her, but his position on the far end of the sofa put a point in the *he-doesn't-like-you-like-that* column.

She set the movie up, hit play, and settled into the couch with her spaghetti—acutely aware of the space between them and how much she longed to cozy up next to his strong body. She quickly brushed the thought away as Bob Newhart appeared on screen.

They watched in silence for the first several minutes. Paige tried to sneak some glances over at Carter to see if he was enjoying it. But as soon as Buddy arrived in New York City, chewing used gum and congratulating the diner on having the best coffee, Carter started letting out a few chuckles. As the movie progressed, he laughed more and more—especially during the scene with Buddy and Santa in the toy store. Paige let out a silent sigh of relief.

"Hey, can you pass me a cookie?" She asked, pointing at the plate on the coffee table in front of Carter.

Carter leaned forward, keeping his eyes glued to the screen, and handed her one. When he settled back into the couch, he had shifted from his original spot, ultimately moving closer to Paige.

I mean, he had to reach over to me to give me the cookie, she thought to herself. *He naturally had to get closer. Don't read into this, Paige.*

She tried to ignore the butterflies in her stomach as she focused back on the movie.

When it got to the scene in Central Park with Jovie singing "Santa Claus is Comin' to Town," Paige snuck another look over at Carter. He seemed entranced by what was happening on the screen. Paige's heart did a backflip.

As the movie wrapped up, she turned to him and asked, "So, what did you think?"

He turned his body toward her and leaned back against the arm of the sofa. He had his hands behind his head and his biceps were trying to steal her attention.

"If I'm being honest," he said, "I came into this pretty skeptical. But I actually really enjoyed it. It was funny, which I liked, and it reminded me a lot of Christmases back in the day with both of my parents. It was nice to experience a little bit of that again."

He gave her a warm and genuine smile.

Damn you, Carter, for being hot and *sensitive.*

"Aww, well, that is really sweet. Now I'm especially glad I picked this one," she replied. "So, was your dad really into Christmas?"

"Yeah, definitely. He'd dress up in a Santa suit and try to make the holiday special for me when I was younger. Since I was an only child, he was always going the extra mile to make things fun around the house," he said as he lowered his arms to cross them over his chest. The position wasn't any less flattering, and he didn't bother pulling down the corner of his shirt, which must have ridden up when his arms were over his head. "Even when I got older he stuck to certain traditions, like picking out our Christmas tree together and making breakfast in bed for my mom on Christmas day. After he died, I didn't really want anything to do with Christmas, or any holiday really, because it was too much of a reminder that he wasn't there anymore. Instead of trying to keep his traditions alive, I just pretended like they never happened at all. Probably wasn't the most mature way to handle things."

It broke Paige's heart to hear him share this. She couldn't imagine a Christmas without both of her parents, and she made a mental note to be extra grateful this year for the time she had with them. She also felt a small pang of guilt for all the over-the-top decorations displayed around them.

"It makes sense that you'd want to do that, though," Paige said. "I'm sure things just didn't feel the same. I can understand why you don't want to get into the Christmas spirit . . . and I'm sorry if I ever crossed the line in pushing it on you."

"No, I'm sorry for overreacting a few weeks ago. I really felt like a jerk after my outburst. I think having been at my mom's house brought up some old memories, and walking in to see all the decorations must have triggered some stuff I haven't been dealing with since he passed away," he confessed. "I really am sorry."

"Don't worry about it," Paige said. "Consider it a hatchet buried."

She held out her hand to him, craving to feel his touch again. His hand met hers for only a second before her cell phone chimed next to her, breaking the brief eye contact they shared.

"Shit," she cursed.

"What's going on?" Carter asked.

"The airline already cancelled tomorrow's flight too. Seems like this storm isn't letting up tonight. I'm rebooked for the 17th, assuming things start to clear up."

As much fun as she was having with Carter, her heart sank when she saw the notification. She missed her parents and had been looking forward to their Christmas traditions.

"That sucks, I'm sorry. I bet you want to get back to your family. And I believe you once said that you couldn't stand to be around me, so I'm sure these past couple of days have been utter torture for you." He winked at her, effectively bringing her mood back up.

"Seriously. I should be awarded a medal or something at the end of all this," she quipped.

"But really," he continued, "I hope the weather chills out soon. What does your family usually do around the holidays?"

Paige told him all about her family traditions—gingerbread house competitions with her cousins, Christmas

Eve walks on the beach making snowmen out of sand, driving around and looking at the lights on the palm trees.

They had had these traditions for as long as she could remember, and with the exception of the one Christmas-time cruise they took when she was twelve, they had never missed a year. She really hoped she wouldn't miss out on all the fun.

"Well, it sounds like you guys always have a good time together," Carter said with a bit of sadness in his eyes. "After my dad passed, I started traveling during Christmas break so I wouldn't need to be around all the reminders. Most trips on my own, one with my mom and Gram, one with—shit, Gram!"

He leapt off the couch and patted his shorts pockets for his phone, finding it nestled in the crack between the arm of the couch and the cushion.

"Sorry," he said in panic. "I was supposed to call my grandmother for her birthday today. I had it in my calendar and everything . . . I'm gonna go call her before it gets too late on the East Coast."

"Yeah, no worries," she assured him as he walked away from the couch. As cute as it was that he needed to call his *Gram*, she couldn't help but feel bummed that their heart-to-heart was cut short.

He was almost at his door when he turned around.

"I guess forgetting to check your calendar is a sign of a day you didn't want distractions from," Carter said, offering another genuine smile before turning back to his room and closing the door.

Paige didn't stop blushing for the rest of the night.

Chapter 14

When Paige woke up the next morning, she could have sworn she had been dreaming of Carter.

The night before had felt like a big shift in their dynamic. Carter continued to open up to her, and she to him. Plus, his last comment to her felt intentional. Why say that if he wasn't starting to feel something for her too? It seemed like a good sign that maybe, just maybe, she wasn't imagining the shift between them.

The snow had finally stopped falling outside, and when she checked the news, she saw that plows were starting to go out and clear the roads. If the weather kept going in this direction, she might be able to fly out tomorrow after all.

Not ready to leave the warmth of her bed, and not sure what to say when she saw Carter, Paige decided to call Nadia.

"Your flight was delayed again?" Nadia asked.

"Yeah, it's looking much better for tomorrow, though," said Paige. "And plus, I don't mind having one more day here."

"Well, it sounds like someone has changed their tune!" Nadia sounded entirely too smug. "This wouldn't have to do with a certain *roommate*, would it?"

"I'm not taking any questions at this time," Paige said, hiding her face behind her pillow.

"Paige! You finally have the hots for Carter, don't you?"

"I mean . . ."

"Spill! Tell me what happened," Nadia demanded.

"Well, you know we had a nice day making cookies, but then he totally ignored me that night," Paige started. "Well, right after I texted you yesterday morning, I went out to the kitchen and he was making me pancakes. Oh, and he even had a fresh coffee ready for me."

"Shut the front door," Nadia said.

"That's not all. I asked him about his attitude the night before and he apologized right away, saying he was in the zone of a workout . . . which I guess I could have deduced from the headphones.

"Of course, you dork," Nadia teased.

"Then after breakfast he challenged me to some Mario Kart, and we ended up playing for like two whole hours. Finally, we put a bet on the last game—which I won—so he had to watch a Christmas movie with me last night."

"Get out."

Now Paige was the one feeling smug. "I'm not making this up. And naturally, I took the decision way too seriously, but I wisely chose *Elf*, and he liked it. He ended up opening up more about his childhood, and then we talked for a little while about our families and Christmas traditions before he realized he forgot to call his grandmother for her birthday—he calls her *Gram*, by the way—so he went back to his room for the rest of the night. But before he turned in, he said the sweetest thing about how good a day it was."

"Okay, what the hell! Why is Carter so freaking romantic all of a sudden?" Nadia exclaimed.

"Nads, I was blushing so hard, and if I hadn't already been sitting, my knees would have buckled out from under me. I don't know how it happened, but I'm crushing *hard* on this guy."

"I mean, it makes sense, Paige. He's essentially a Greek god who apparently isn't afraid to share his emotions. How could anyone resist that kind of charm?"

"I mean, why the change, though? And isn't it all too good to be true? I was nervous that the crush might be one-sided, but after his comment last night, I have to imagine he feels *something*," Paige said. "I just can't help but wonder what the catch is . . . What am I missing? Am I just another girl he's trying to get into bed with? I really don't want to be some rebound to help him get over an ex."

"What if there is no catch?" Nadia asked. "What if he really is a good guy who deserves a chance?"

"I know, I know, I just don't want to end up getting hurt again." Paige sighed.

"Of course you don't," Nadia said. "But if you go through life avoiding any possible sign of danger, you'll only end up hurting yourself. Trust me, I don't want a repeat of Chance either, but I also don't want you to stay hiding behind all of this armor. You are capable, smart, and funny, and with or without a man, I just want to see you be the version of *you* who doesn't live in fear."

"Have I told you how much I love you?" Paige said. "If Linus hadn't scooped you up, I would be first in line."

"Well, then you can get next dibs," Nadia joked. "So, if Carter is moving out at the beginning of January and you leave for California tomorrow, then today might be your last chance to tell him how you feel. Are you gonna do it?

"I don't know. I'll see what the vibes are like when I head out there and play it by ear," Paige said. "But wait! No proposal yet?"

"Not yet," Nadia answered. "But with the roads clearing up a bit today, Linus has been pushing for us to go out toward the lake. So I have a hunch it's imminent."

Paige knew her friend well enough to know that Nadia had a huge smile on her face. And she couldn't be happier for her.

"Okay, well, you need to keep me updated if *anything* happens," Paige demanded.

"Oh, don't worry, I'll text you before I even say yes, like I promised. Linus will understand," Nadia said. "Speak of the devil, he just poked his head in the room. He looks antsy. I'm gonna hang up now. Text you later, love you!"

"Love you too!" Paige hung up and finally got herself out of bed. She spent a little extra time in front of the mirror getting ready before heading out to see Carter.

When Paige walked out into the common space of the condo, it was quiet.

Carter must still be asleep, she thought.

But then she noticed the door to his room was cracked open.

"Carter?" she called out, walking toward his door.

She gave the door a small nudge as she called out his name again. No reply. As she stood in his doorway, she caught the scent of his cologne and lingered longer than she meant to.

Paige had never seen the inside of the room after Carter moved in. For a room that belonged to a man, it was surprisingly tidy and minimalist. A stark contrast to Chance's room, which had band memorabilia on every inch of the walls and clothes piled up in the corner.

As she gave Carter's room a scan, she noticed a wrapped Christmas gift on his desk.

The edges were perfectly smooth, and the bow looked almost professional. *Either Carter is freakishly good at wrapping or he asked a store clerk for help*, she thought to herself.

Just then, Paige heard Carter's now-familiar bellowing laugh coming from outside the window. She left his room and walked to the living room window and looked out onto the street. There on the sidewalk, shovel in hand, was a bundled-up Carter with their elderly neighbor, Carol. Carter was helping her clear the driveway of her house now that the blizzard had stopped.

Paige's heart was effectively melted. She snapped a photo and sent it to Nadia.

> Look at where I just found Carter . . .

> Is he helping Carol shovel snow?? Paige, you've got to lock this guy down lol.

Paige put her phone in her pocket and bundled up to join them.

***

"Well, well, well," Carter said as Paige came out of the front door, shovel in hand. "Look who finally decided to come help." He gave her a wink.

"How long have you been out here?" she asked. "It's freezing!"

"We started around nine-thirty, then popped inside Carol's place for some coffee after about thirty minutes because we could barely feel our hands. Now we're back at it."

"Paige, you didn't tell me you had this nice young man hiding away in there," Carol commented excitedly. "He so kindly offered to help me this morning when he noticed me slipping around the driveway."

"We can't have you falling out here in the freezing cold now, Carol." Carter smiled, even though his tone had turned more serious.

Paige couldn't help but smile too. "Well, put me to work! Let's get you a clear driveway."

Carter and Paige began shoveling piles of snow off of Carol's driveway and sidewalk.

"So, what have you two been chatting about?" Paige asked.

"Carol was telling me about her glory days here in Chicago," Carter said. "I asked her about what she used to do for work, how long she's lived in this house, about her family. I must say, I had no idea we lived next door to such a legend."

"Well, Carol is the best neighbor we could have asked for," Paige called out. "Is your daughter coming this year, Carol?"

"She's supposed to," Carol replied. "But this weather has really messed up everyone's plans. She's hoping she can make the drive here tomorrow."

"Tell me about it," Paige groaned. "Well, hopefully she can make it now that the snow is slowing down. Looks like my flight to California is scheduled to go out tomorrow too."

"Oh yeah?" Carter's head snapped up, and he locked eyes with her from across the driveway. "I mean, that's good. You'll get to be with your parents after all."

He forced a smile, but Paige could have sworn the look in his eyes was one of disappointment.

"Carter was telling me about the fun you guys have been getting up to," said Carol, stealing Paige's glance. "Said he never had this much fun with—"

"Man, is it cold!" Carter interrupted. "Carol, are you sure you don't want to wait inside while Paige and I finish up out here?"

Now Carter had a panicked look on his face as he set his shovel down and walked Carol by the arm back toward her front door. Paige was confused by Carter's blatant interruption but decided to keep on shoveling. It was probably best for Carol not to be outside anyway.

Carter returned a minute later and joined her.

"I'd hate to see her catch a cold before her daughter and her family get here. Best for her to stay warm inside," Carter stated.

"Yeah, definitely. How's your Gram, by the way? I hope she had a nice birthday."

"She's great. Seventy-seven but still sharp as a whip." He beamed. "She tried giving me a hard time for calling so late, so I blamed it on you."

He nudged her with his shoulder as he said it, not realizing Paige was standing on a patch of hidden ice. She lost her balance and fell into the pile of snow she had just shoveled.

"Oh shit," Carter swore. "I'm so sorry, I didn't mean for that to happen. Here, let me help you."

He held out his gloved hand for her. As he tried pulling her up, his foot slipped on the same patch of ice and he toppled forward on top of her.

They both started laughing as they situated themselves in the snowbank to face each other. If their faces hadn't already been flushed from the cold, they would have been rosy from blushing.

They laid there, staring into each other's eyes for what felt like an eternity. Paige's body didn't even register the cold temperature anymore. She felt like she was radiating heat being this close to Carter.

The next thing Paige knew, she was leaning in toward him.

Wait, what am I doing? She panicked. *I didn't think this through. Is it too late to pull back?*

But before she could change course, Carter's lips met hers.

They were soft and warm, and they sent butterflies through her entire body.

If this is what a kiss was meant to feel like, she had been doing it all wrong.

Then, as quickly as the kiss happened, it was interrupted by Carol's voice from the front door.

"Are you two okay? It looks awfully slippery out there," she bellowed.

Carter gave Paige a smile before pushing himself up.

"All good over here, Carol! Couldn't be better," Carter replied, brushing the snow off his coat.

Paige got up on her feet and called out, "This is why we're out here instead of you!"

They resumed their shoveling, sneaking looks at each other every couple of minutes.

Paige's mind was racing. *Was that going to happen again, or did he just feel caught up in the moment? I'm his landlord! Did he enjoy that kiss as much as I did? I'm not making this up, he keeps looking over here, right? My god, Paige, chill! I really need some dating practice.*

As they finished up, Carol walked out on the porch to say thank you and Merry Christmas. Paige and Carter waved goodbye and shuffled in silence across the icy street back into the warmth of the condo.

Once they got out of their snow gear, Paige was the first to speak. "So, you want a hot chocolate?"

"Yeah, that sounds great," he said, rubbing his hands together as he sat down at the island. "So—"

"That was really nice of you to help Carol today," Paige said, accidentally interrupting whatever Carter was about to say. "Sorry, I didn't mean to—"

"It's okay," Carter assured her. "And it was nothing—just being a good neighbor. I was up early working on something and luckily I heard some commotion outside and looked out the window. I would hate for her to have to do that all by herself. It *was* pretty icy . . ."

She could feel his eyes burning into her as he said it.

"Was it? I didn't notice," Paige joked, though she couldn't bring herself to look at Carter. "Look, about that . . . icy patch . . . I hope I didn't make you uncomfortable or anything. I don't really know where that came fro—"

"Paige," Carter interjected. "You only beat me to it."

God, she loved hearing him say her name. She gave in and finally met his gaze.

He smiled that Hollywood smile at her and continued, "I've been wanting to do that for a couple of days now, but I didn't want to make things weird if you didn't feel the same way."

So, he was flirting.

"Okay, well, great!" she responded, realizing she sounded a little too enthusiastic. "Glad we've established that it's not weird."

Nice, Paige. Now you really are making it weird.

"I guess we have." Carter smirked.

As they finished their hot cocoa, all Paige could think about was how badly she wanted to kiss him again, but she decided to play it cool.

"I'm about to venture out to the grocery store to grab some things for dinner tonight and breakfast tomorrow. Want to join me?" she asked.

Right as she asked, Carter's phone chimed. When he looked down at his new text message, his facial expression changed from relaxed to solemn. He spent a few seconds rereading the message before looking back up, his smile back in place—albeit a bit forced.

"Sorry, you said grocery store? Yeah, why not." He got up and made his way around the island to drop his mug in the sink.

Before he walked back to the front door, he stopped behind her. Paige could feel the warmth of his body at her back, heating her own body in more ways than one. He tucked a few loose strands of her hair behind her ear, bent down and whispered, "Would hate for you to slip on the ice again without me there to fall behind you."

Paige's knees were weak, and she grasped on tighter to the countertop to make sure she didn't melt into the floor.

After regaining her composure, she took inventory of the near-empty kitchen, bundled back up, and followed Carter out the door.

She couldn't help feeling a twinge of anxiety in her stomach. She wasn't sure if it was the fact that she feared she was out of her depth with Carter or the look on his face when he got that text. Not to mention the fact that he was moving out soon and might pretend like this never happened. Maybe it was all the above. But she pushed the feeling aside and stepped out into the cold Chicago air.

Chapter 15

"I can't believe you've never tried deep-dish pizza," Paige said, perplexed. "That's like, one of the first things Nadia and I did when we moved here."

"You forget that I'm from the East Coast. I grew up an hour outside of New York City, so the only pizza that I choose to recognize is a thin-crust slice bigger than my face," Carter stated. "Whatever that saucy dish is, it most definitely is not pizza."

The pair had returned from the store and were putting away their groceries. Paige bought fixings for them to have a charcuterie board, including a brie that she planned to bake with honey and walnuts. She threw in a few extra snacks to have on her plane ride, plus a couple of bottles of wine. She hoped some liquid courage might help her tell Carter how she really felt about him before the night was over.

Carter bought a few frozen thin-crust pizzas and some more protein bars to hold himself over until the snow cleared and he could resume his usual takeout routine.

While they were shopping they talked about their favorite spots in Chicago, favorite places they've traveled to, and crazy stories from their early twenties.

Talking to Carter was comfortable—something Paige hadn't experienced in a long time. The more she got to know him, the more she saw how funny and sensitive he really was. He was the opposite of how he'd originally presented himself to be. And she was dying to better understand what had changed.

After putting the groceries away, they each retreated to their own rooms to shower before dinner.

The warm water felt like a blanket surrounding Paige's skin. After spending all that time out shoveling and walking to the grocery store, she was chilled to her bones. The only thing that kept her from soaking in a hot bath was the fact that Carter would be waiting for her in the kitchen.

Once she was dry, Paige wasn't sure what to wear. Typically, she would go with something cozy and comfortable, but now that she knew Carter was interested in her, she didn't want to look like a total slob.

She settled on leggings with a cute yet slightly oversized Christmas sweater. She followed it up by putting on mascara and some subtle lip gloss. She figured this elevated her comfy look a little bit.

"How many Christmas sweaters do you own?" Carter questioned her when she walked out of her room.

"Nadia and I get new ones each year, so at this point we each have about eight or nine," Paige replied proudly.

"Well, you're nothing if not dedicated," Carter said. He was leaning against the island in a black T-shirt and black joggers, giving Paige a half smile that sent her head spinning. "Are you excited to get back home tomorrow?"

"Yeah, I am," Paige confessed. "Don't get me wrong, these last couple of days have actually been much better than I thought they'd be, but I hate the thought of missing Christmas with my family."

"I get that," he said. "It's going to feel lonely here, but I really hope your flight can go out tomorrow."

He gave her a genuine smile before grabbing one of the wine bottles and pouring them each a glass.

Paige started getting the charcuterie board ready for their dinner.

"So," she started, "what *were* you going to do this Christmas anyway? You said you usually travel somewhere?"

"Absolutely nothing," he answered. "For the first time in five years, I was planning to do this." He pointed around the condo. "Just sit at home and chill. Lately I've packed so much into my life to try to avoid feeling anything too intensely." He paused and took a drink of his wine. "It's always been my coping mechanism—even before my dad passed—and losing him only made it more necessary. The more I stood still, the more I missed him, so I decided I would just constantly be moving and chase the highs so I didn't need to experience the lows."

"Wow, it's great that you're so self-aware," Paige said. She was genuinely impressed.

"Well, after so many years of running from my emotions, I finally hit the wall," Carter admitted. "I went to see a therapist and he helped me sort through all of this shit in my head. I finally saw that everything in my life was superficial. The way I dressed, the way I acted, the way I lived, the vacations I took, the apartment I lived in, my friendships, my relationships—none of it actually made me happy long-term. So, I went against every instinct in my body that told me to just deal with it and stay numb, and I finally decided to make some changes."

Is this what a real adult relationship looks like? She thought to herself. *I don't think Chance ever had a thought this profound—at least nothing he ever said out loud.*

Paige reached across the island and squeezed his hand. "For what it's worth, I don't see anything superficial about you. All I see is a kind and genuine man who expresses his feelings, helps elderly neighbors in need, and really, really sucks at Mario Kart."

"Well, wait a minute now." He gasped playfully. "That race was mine to win and you know it."

"Whatever helps you sleep at night, Carter."

"Stupid blue shell," he muttered under his breath.

Paige's phone timer went off, and she took her hand out of his grasp. She grabbed the baked brie from the oven and brought the completed cheeseboard over to the coffee table. Carter followed behind her with both their glasses of wine and the open bottle.

They situated themselves on the couch—this time sitting much closer to each other. Paige's heart skipped a beat.

"So, you said you've made some changes. Anything new in your dating life?" Paige asked boldly, admittedly a bit nervous to hear his answer.

Carter took a sip of his wine.

"My last relationship never went below surface level. She's an aspiring model and I'm a little ashamed to admit that I started dating her because she fit with what I thought my life should look like." Carter had the decency to look uncomfortable with this admission, but didn't hold back as he continued. "We went to fancy parties and traveled to exotic places, which helped numb the grief of losing my dad. But we never talked about anything important. I was okay with it for so long because our lifestyles were a good fit and the physical part of our relationship was never an issue." He shrugged as if he were sharing the most casual detail. "But eventually, I couldn't deny any longer that I felt hollow." Carter's gaze lifted to meet Paige's briefly before he grabbed a cracker and a slice of cheese.

Paige was trying not to spiral. Carter's life had looked exactly as she'd imagined it when she first met him. "How recent was this?" She couldn't help but ask the question. She saw a brief look of panic on his face, and she feared her suspicions about a recent breakup were true.

"We started dating about three years ago," Carter said, not fully answering the question. "And then, uh, we bro—"

Paige's phone went off. It was Nadia trying to Face-Time.

"Oh my god," Paige exclaimed. "I think Nadia just got engaged! Do you mind if I answer?"

"Not at all, let's see the bling," he said, looking relieved.

As soon as Paige answered the call, she saw Nadia's left hand directly in front of the camera with a diamond ring on her finger.

"Guess who's gonna be Mrs. Eriksson!" She exclaimed.

Paige let out a shriek of excitement for her friend.

Nadia filled her in on the events of their day. She and Linus drove out to the lake to take a walk. They came across a bench and sat down to take in the view of the icy water. When Nadia turned to look at Linus, he was sitting there, ring in his cold, purple hand, and then he asked her to marry him.

Nadia said that Linus had all these other elaborate ideas in mind, and the blizzard had thwarted all of them. But to her, this was the most romantic proposal she could have asked for—just the two of them taking in the view of the lake and the city they both now called home.

They talked for a few more minutes until Nadia had to go to start making calls to her family. Paige was honored to have been the first FaceTime.

"They look so happy," Paige said to Carter after hanging up. She reached over and filled their wine glasses up with what was left in the bottle, completely forgetting where she and Carter had left off in their conversation.

"Yeah, they really do," Carter agreed, but kept his eyes down on his glass. "So, what about you? Ever gotten close to getting married?"

"I thought I was close with my ex from work," Paige confided. "But turns out I was the only one who thought that. We dated for just over three years, and the way we talked, I thought we had a future together. But looking back on it now, I realize he never really gave me anything aside from empty promises." She took a gulp of wine. "You know, he even had the nerve to come begging for forgiveness after he cheated on me. And in less than two weeks, his head was already turned back to the other girl."

"Real class act." Carter rolled his eyes.

"For the past year I've avoided dating. I think part of me just didn't want to open myself up to getting hurt again, but if I'm being really introspective, I think a big part of me feels like I just won't be enough for anyone. I wasn't enough for Chance to propose. Hell, I was barely enough to meet his family more than a few times. And do you know how humiliating it is for someone to cheat on you? Like, as if I needed a bigger reason to feel unwanted."

Paige surprised even herself with this revelation. There was something about Carter that made her feel more in tune with her emotions. She felt safe putting her thoughts out in the open.

"Chance is an absolute idiot," Carter said, reaching over and grabbing her wine-free hand. "I've only known you a few weeks, and I only really started getting to know you a couple of days ago, but you're special, Paige. You have passions, you have personality, you have depth. You have this way of making me feel one hundred percent comfortable with you, which is something I haven't experienced in a long, long time. I need you to understand that you are most definitely wanted."

Carter had scooted himself closer to her while he was talking, and Paige's body was tingling more with each centimeter of the gap he closed between them.

He was like a magnet, because Paige realized she was already leaning into him, practically begging for him to kiss her. But as soon as he finished his sentence he was there, meeting her lips again with the same softness from earlier.

The kiss lasted longer than before, but they eventually parted and Carter rested his forehead against hers.

Paige's heart was pounding so hard she was sure Carter could hear it. She never believed it when people said they experienced fireworks during a kiss, but now she had firsthand proof.

"I know we're snowed in here," he breathed, "but I still feel like I can't get enough of you."

And with that, they were kissing again, this time with more passion. Carter's right hand moved to her thigh, his left hand lightly resting on her neck with his thumb stroking her jawline.

Paige grabbed at his T-shirt and used it to pull herself even closer to him. The next thing she knew she was tugging his shirt up, and he obliged by pulling it up and over his head, breaking their kiss just enough for her to give his chiseled torso a once-over.

He wrapped his arms around her, effectively pulling her into his lap. If he couldn't hear her heart before, there was no way he couldn't hear it now. He traced his fingers down her back, and Paige felt electricity surge through her body. This was the hottest thing that had happened to her in a long time—maybe ever—and her pulse was racing.

It was clear Carter knew what he was doing. The movement of his tongue was skillful and subtle, and his hands touched all the right places. Paige started to worry her hookup drought would become obvious to him. Did she still remember the right techniques? Was he enjoying this as much as she was?

"What's wrong? Do you want to stop?" he asked, sensing her hesitation.

Why am I overthinking this?

Paige wanted this. She wanted *him.*

"No," she whispered. She pulled her sweater over her head and pulled him toward her as she laid back on the couch.

***

"That was . . ." Paige's brain couldn't come up with the words to adequately describe the sex she just had.

"Amazing?" Carter finished her sentence.

"What's better than amazing?" She smirked as she ran her hand through his hair, twirling a strand around her finger.

He tilted his head up to kiss her again as she laid on his chest.

"Are you *sure* your flight tomorrow didn't get delayed?" Carter asked jokingly. "I'm not ready to let you go." He wrapped his arms around her and stroked her back.

"Well, you're not making it easy, that's for certain," she murmured against his chest.

"Fine," he conceded. "I'll be waiting patiently for your return then."

"You know," she said, "if I'm leaving tomorrow, we should probably go for round two to hold ourselves over."

"Consider my attention piqued." With one arm already wrapped around her, Carter used his other to roll her over so he was on top of her.

They made love again—this time was even better than the first—and then stayed up talking until they couldn't stay awake any longer, falling asleep to the beat of each other's hearts.

***

ang, bang, bang.

Paige slowly opened her eyes as she realized someone was knocking on her door. She checked her phone: 8:27 a.m.

Bang, bang, bang.

Who could possibly be at the door at this hour? She thought, still half asleep.

She smiled at the still-groggy Carter as she got up off the couch. She threw on her leggings and sweater and made her way to the front door.

Paige opened it to find the most beautiful woman with dark hair and perfectly symmetrical features standing opposite her.

"Hi, can I help you?" Paige asked the mystery woman.

"Yeah," she said, sounding annoyed. "I'm looking for my boyfriend."

Chapter 16

Paige stared at the woman on the other side of the door for a few seconds before responding. She was still half asleep and felt like she must have misunderstood this unwanted visitor.

"I'm sorry," Paige started, "I'm confused. You're looking for who?"

"My boyfriend," she said with a deadpan expression. "Carter Kinney."

Paige's heart dropped to her stomach. Surely this was some kind of joke.

She was frozen in place, face white as a ghost.

"Carter. Kinney?" the woman repeated herself, looking more impatient if that were possible.

Paige was still frozen, trying to wrap her head around what she was seeing and hearing. *Beautiful woman. Boyfriend. Carter. How could that be right?*

"Monica?" Carter's voice filled the doorway. "Wha—what are you doing here?"

Paige hadn't even noticed Carter come up behind her.

"You asshole!" Monica took a step toward him and smacked her hand on his chest. "So, you're really not going to return any of my messages? Or say thank you for the gift? That watch was expensive, you know."

"Monica, we talked about this," he hissed. "I thought I made it perfectly clear the other night. And please take the gift back. You know full well I haven't even opened it."

So that explains the perfectly wrapped gift I saw on Carter's desk, and likely why he was in such a bad mood the night before the blizzard.

"Who the hell is this?" Monica pointed at Paige, who finally snapped out of her state of shock.

Carter had stepped in front of Paige now, shielding her from Monica's fury.

"What? Oh, this is my roommate, Paige," he replied.

My roommate. The words were like a slap in the face to Paige. *There is no way you do the things we did last night to someone who is just your roommate.*

"You expect me to believe you went and got a roommate?" She snickered. "Tell me, Carter, are you in the middle of making her daddy's precious pancakes right now?"

She knows about Carter's breakfast move. Of course that's all this was to him. One big move to get me into bed.

Paige was fuming now.

"Stop this, Monica," Carter said sternly. He turned to her. "I'm so sorry about this, Paige."

"Don't," Paige snapped.

"I am *not* in a relationship with Monica," he insisted, shooting a glare back toward the door where the woman in question still stood. "We broke up back in October. You have to believe me."

Paige rolled her eyes and stormed past him back toward her bedroom.

"Paige, wait," Carter pleaded, but she didn't turn back around.

Her head was spinning as she entered her room and slammed the door. *All this time he's had a girlfriend? Here I was worried about being a rebound, when I actually needed to worry about being the* other *woman.*

Her ears were ringing, and she hoped if she laid down and put a pillow over her head, it would make it all stop. She could barely make out Carter arguing with Monica.

"I told you I was done, Monica. I didn't mean we need a break. We needed to *break up*. I thought my moving out sent a pretty obvious message."

"Oh, come on, Carter, you're being dramatic. We go together. I mean, just look at us."

"Me, dramatic? We both know I've never been the dramatic one."

"Well, when you're done playing with your shiny new toy, you can come back home ... You'll be bored with her soon enough. But I expect you to be groveling when you return."

"Don't hold your breath. On the other hand, do. I really don't care. We're done."

Paige heard the slam of a door followed by the chime of her phone. A notification from the airline confirming today's flight was still on time.

Thank god, she thought. *I need to get out of here ASAP.*

She opened her messaging app, sent a scathing text about Carter over to Nadia, and threw her phone down on her bed. She then moved her mostly packed suitcase to her bed and started frantically throwing in last-minute essentials.

Paige had meant to finish the night before, but when things with Carter heated up, it was the last thing on her mind.

Why did you sleep with him, Paige? She asked herself. *Of course it was too good to be true. Just another scumbag who cheats on his girlfriend.*

As if on cue, Carter knocked on her door. "Paige, you have to let me explain."

"Explain what?" Paige asked without going to the door. "The fact that you have a girlfriend? The fact that you conveniently forgot to mention her to me before you got me into bed? I mean, come on, Carter, she knows your big move. I can't believe I was so stupid not to see that you were playing me."

"It's not like that. She is *not* my girlfriend," he insisted, still yelling through the closed door. "Can I *please* come in?"

Paige paused her packing and looked at the door. She figured she'd just get the conversation over with while she was still angry and could give Carter a piece of her mind. So she made her way to the door and opened it to a crestfallen Carter on the other side.

The second the door opened, he took a step forward.

"Monica is not my girlfriend anymore, I swear," he blurted out. "Like I started to say last night, we were dating for three years, and we started living together six months ago. I knew I shouldn't have moved in at the time because my heart wasn't in it, but I was too chicken to say anything until a couple of months ago. I agreed to go on a break, even when I knew I was done. I just didn't think she would try so hard to get back together. I figured she'd just forget about me and move on to the next guy who gave her attention."

"And you didn't have the balls to actually end it then?" She couldn't look him in the eye as she threw the last items into her suitcase.

"Well, no, it's just tha—"

Ding.

Paige's phone interrupted Carter's rebuttal.

He looked down instinctively after hearing the chime to see her phone open on her chat with Nadia.

He must have seen a few words from the exchange.

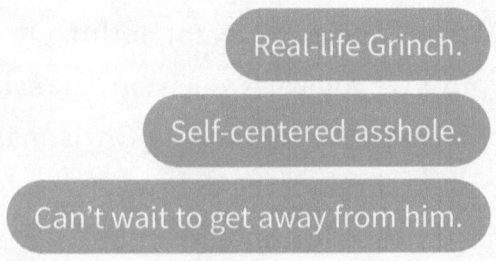

"Wow," Carter said, rolling his eyes. "Couldn't even give me two seconds to explain myself before talking shit about me? That's real mature."

"Well, maybe you deserved it," Paige said defensively.

She knew as soon as she said it that it wasn't fair, but she was too angry to care.

"Give me that." Paige snatched the phone from where it was lying on the bed. "And what do you care what I think, anyway? I'm just your *roommate*, right?"

"I didn't mean it like that, and you know it," he bit back.

"The only thing I know is that when I get back from California, you and all of your things better be gone." She was fuming.

Paige could see the pain in Carter's eyes, and deep down she believed his intentions were good, but she was filled with too much rage to be rational. Everything about this situation with Monica brought Paige right back to last year with Chance, but this time *she* was the other woman.

"Well, it's clear you want nothing to do with me, so I'll happily give you what you want," he said as he headed out of her room. "Merry fucking Christmas," he grumbled as he passed through the doorway.

Paige heard his door slam a few seconds later as she was calling a rideshare.

She finished packing the last of her things and went outside to get into her Uber to the airport. She was going to be four hours early, but she couldn't bear the thought of spending another second in the condo with Carter.

Yet, she couldn't stop thinking about the situation the entire car ride. Paige felt like she had been made a fool of again. She was so angry with him for playing her—for not being completely honest with her before they slept together. The more she replayed everything in her mind, the more she realized how many opportunities he had to bring up Monica. Even if he was telling the truth about them not being together anymore, it was still so recent. She deserved to know—especially before taking things to the level they had the night before.

Paige had come to believe Carter was different from other guys. Their dynamic had felt so different and so right. And as mad as she was, she was also sad, too, to lose something that seemed special.

She closed her eyes and rested her head against the window.

In a few hours I'll be wheels up and will never have to see this prick again.

The thought gave her some solace, but she couldn't shake the pit in her stomach.

Chapter 17

F ive days came and went, but not even the San Diego sun could cheer up Paige's spirits.

She was grateful to be around her parents, aunts, uncles, and cousins, but she couldn't stop thinking about Carter—even during her family's annual gingerbread house decorating competition. Her thoughts bounced between anger at his deception, to missing being around him.

Their days snowed in together had brought Paige more joy than she had had in a long time. Carter was good-looking, but also sensitive, kind, and funny. She hadn't felt like that around a guy in ages—not even with Chance.

But that didn't change the fact that he had lied about having ties to another woman—someone who clearly believed they weren't well and truly over.

Monica thought she was still in a relationship with him, but what does going on a break really mean? He seemed so sincere about being done with their relationship. Maybe I shouldn't have been so quick to shut him out . . .

As Paige put the final touches on her gingerbread house, she couldn't help but wonder what would have happened if Monica had never showed up at her door. Would Carter have stayed, or would he have still moved out? Would he have asked her out on an actual date or would they have slept together a couple more times and then never spoken again? She wanted to believe the spark between them was real, but she didn't know what to trust at the moment.

Those last few days with Carter had taught Paige two things: one, she was terrified of opening up her heart again. She had been so blindsided by Chance's betrayal that she shut out the thought of love and happily ever after. She had been so sure he was the one, but her trust had been shattered.

And two, as scared as she was, she *wanted* to open up her heart. The connection she had with Carter was undeniable. It just felt right. He felt like a piece of her puzzle that she had been missing. In hindsight, she could see that Chance was a piece that didn't quite fit—as hard as she tried to make it work. But something about Carter made her feel seen, appreciated, and whole. Those days snowed in together made her realize a relationship like that could add to her life and make her stronger.

She placed her last gumdrop on the gingerbread roof and brought her house to the dining table alongside the rest of her family. Hers was nowhere near the best this year—as if her mind had been elsewhere the entire time.

***

It was already sixty degrees when Paige woke up on Christmas Eve morning, and by the time her family left for their beach walk, it was sixty-six. Her family members layered up with long sleeves and jackets, but having acclimated to Chicago weather, Paige was happy in a light pullover and vest.

Each year they picked a different beach for their walk, and this year was Torrey Pines State Beach. They grabbed some warm drinks from Bird Rock Coffee Roasters on their way and set off for an easy stroll after nabbing the last parking spot along the beach.

"Oh, Paige," her mom, Anne, started, "we just saw Nadia's announcement on Facebook! How wonderful that she and Linus are getting married!"

Though Paige was the first to find out about Nadia and Linus's engagement, they had decided to wait a few days before making a public announcement so they could tell other friends and family first.

"I know," Paige said, smiling at the joy on Nadia's face when she FaceTimed her. "I'm over the moon for them."

As a means to distract herself from thinking about Carter, and because she was genuinely excited for her friend, Paige had spent her entire flight to San Diego browsing Pinterest for ideas to send to Nadia. It was worth the seven dollars spent on Wi-Fi.

Paige wondered how long it would take her mom to start prying into her own love life.

"How's the dating scene in Chicago?"

Apparently not that long, Paige thought.

"You know, there's a new guy who just started at my firm who is cute. I can ask him if he's single," her mom said.

Her mom was an administrator at an investment firm in San Diego. Retirement had gotten a bit too boring for Anne, and this admin role kept her entertained during the week.

"Oh my gosh, mom," Paige replied, rolling her eyes. "Even if that wasn't utterly humiliating, you do remember I live halfway across the country, right?"

Paige shuddered at the thought of having her mom ask out a man on her behalf. But she decided to confide in her about her current dating predicament.

"If you must know, I'm thinking of getting back out there soon. I feel ready. You know how I told you about my roommate?"

"The standoffish one with the handsome face?"

"Yeah, wait, how do you know he's handsome? I nev—oh my god, you Facebook stalked him, didn't you?" Paige already knew the answer.

"What else are moms supposed to do?" Anne said.

Paige couldn't help but laugh.

"Yes, my handsome *and rude* roommate. He was terrible at first. I could barely stand to be in the room with him, he was that bad. But when we were snowed in together, he actually turned out to be a pretty nice guy, and I developed a major crush," Paige admitted, leaving out the part about their steamy romantic evening to spare herself from her mother's reaction.

"Well, you should ask him on a date!" her mom exclaimed.

"It's . . . complicated." Paige sighed. "He just got out of a relationship, and I don't want to be his easy rebound." She decided to keep the backstory short and sweet, partly because she didn't feel like explaining the difference between a break and breakup to her mother, but mostly because it still stung to think about how Carter didn't bother telling her about Monica.

"That's not always a bad thing, you know," Anne offered. "Your dad and I met right after I broke up with my ex-boyfriend, but I never thought of him as a rebound. I was all in right from the start."

"Wait, really?" Paige asked. "I don't think I ever knew that."

"Oh yeah, I had dated so many boring guys, and this boyfriend was no different," Anne explained. "He worked for Grandpa, so I felt like I had to stick it out with him because of that. But you can't force a spark, hon. I called it off and he was devastated, but I knew he wasn't the guy for me. And then just a couple of weeks later, I met your dad at a concert, and it was love at first sight."

"I knew about the concert story, but I had no idea you were only recently single." Paige loved the story of her parents' meet-cute. Each time she heard it, it renewed her belief in true love.

"You never know when love will knock on your door! If you really like this guy, and if you think he might like you too, just talk to him when you go back to Chicago." Her mom gave her a reassuring smile.

"Thanks, mom. I really needed that," Paige said as the pair stepped back in stride with the rest of the group.

At the end of their walk, the family piled into the car and went on a hunt for the best Christmas lights in the city. And for the first time in six days, Paige was filled with Christmas cheer.

Chapter 18

T he sun peeked through the blinds of Paige's childhood bedroom on Christmas morning, and the
smell of fresh coffee pulled her out of bed and toward
the kitchen where her early riser dad was surely getting
started on breakfast.

They always started Christmas morning with a big
meal, and when she turned into the kitchen, she saw a
box of pancake mix sitting on the counter. She couldn't
help but smile as she thought of Carter.

"Hey, dad, let me help," she said, grabbing a mixing
bowl and the rest of the pancake ingredients. "I learned
a trick recently to make the best pancakes."

Paige added in the ingredients just as Carter had
taught her the week before, carefully mixing everything
together. She poured the batter onto the pan and within
minutes she had a beautiful stack of golden pancakes to
set in front of her dad, Ron.

"Whatever trick you used, I need to learn it! These are fantastic, Paige," he said.

"You just need to pay attention to the little things," Paige said, echoing Carter's words. "You need to put the ingredients in the bowl in the right order, don't mix them too fast, and take your time before the first flip on the pan."

"Well, compliments to the chef, and the chef's teacher," Ron replied before digging back into his pancakes.

Paige started on the next stack as her mom filed into the kitchen. She had thought a lot about what her mom had told her the day before, and the pancake mix on the counter this morning felt like a sign.

She knew she should have given Carter more time to tell her his side of the story before she jumped to conclusions. Paige was still hurt by his lack of communication about his relationship status with Monica, especially after she told him about her past with Chance, but what if he was really feeling the same thing she was feeling? On the flip side, what if her blatant rejection of his apology sent him straight back into the arms of his ex-girlfriend? Being alone at the holidays sucked—she knew from personal experience the year before—and as cool as Carter portrayed himself, Paige knew he wasn't immune to feeling lonely. Besides, he had seen the messages she sent to Nadia. He probably thought she wanted nothing to do with him anymore.

Paige decided she would ask Carter to meet up as soon as she got back to Chicago so she could apologize for the messages and talk through everything that happened, and she desperately hoped he would say yes.

***

After breakfast, the family moved on to opening presents.

Paige gave each of her parents the books she got them on Black Friday.

She unwrapped a candle, a sweater, some fun nail polish, and a gift certificate to upgrade her Nespresso machine when she got back to Chicago.

She thought of the first morning snowed in with Carter and how he stole her freshly brewed coffee. It had infuriated her in the moment, but she couldn't help but smile at the memory now. If she had told herself eleven days ago that she would be missing Carter, she would have laughed out loud. But here she was, wishing she could be wrapped up in his arms.

As they were cleaning up at the end of the gift exchange, there was a knock on the door.

The family exchanged confused glances, clearly not expecting company on the holiday. Paige was closest to the front door, so she made her way over to it.

Dad probably just forgot about something he ordered for mom. But I didn't think they delivered on holidays.

When she opened the door, her stomach flipped, and she let out an audible gasp.

Standing there on the front porch was Carter, decked out in the ugliest Christmas sweater she had ever seen.

"What the—"

"Hi," Carter said at the same time, interrupting Paige's shocked response.

She blinked several times to confirm that this wasn't a dream.

"Hi," she said back, smiling from ear to ear. "What are you doing here? How did you know where to find me?"

She looked into his golden-brown eyes, still in shock that he was standing right in front of her.

"I just couldn't get past how we left things last week," Carter confessed. "And I couldn't stand the thought that I might not see you again without getting another chance to apologize."

Paige had thought about that too. Carter was set to move out the first week of January, and she was nervous he would be gone by the time she got back to the condo.

"Are you kidding?" Paige interjected. "It's me who should be apologizing to you! I shouldn't have sent those messages about you, and I should have given you a fair chance to explain yourself. I'm so sorry I shut you out."

"Well, it was actually those messages that helped me figure out where to find you," he said. "I was just moping around the condo wishing I could see you and talk to you, but I thought that if I tried to call or text you would ignore the message. Besides, a call or text felt like too small of a gesture. That's when I got the idea to reach out to Nadia. Shortly after I moved in, Nadia found me on Instagram and sent me a follow request that I ignored."

Super subtle, Nadia.

"So, I went back to the app, accepted her request, and sent her a message. I asked if she thought you'd be okay with a surprise visit after everything that happened, and where to find you. I knew I could wait for you to get back, but with each minute that passed, it felt like I was losing my grip on the one thing I've cared about in a long time."

Paige couldn't believe the effort he had put into this. Any thought of him playing her had gone out the window the moment she found him on the other side of the door, because this was a move she had only seen in the movies.

"Well, I'm very glad you're here." She smiled. "And by the way, you're looking quite . . . festive."

"Oh, this old thing? I figured I'd really give my apology visit 110% effort," Carter said. "I know I said that all of your Christmas stuff was the stupidest thing I had ever seen, but then I realized the stupidest thing I had seen was me walking out of your room that day without fighting for a chance. Paige, you are funny, determined, smart, hot as hell, and optimistic even when life throws you curveball after curveball. I've been a coward and I've led a shallow existence the last several years, afraid to feel too much because I didn't want to lose another person I cared about. But getting to know you makes that impossible. You make me want to feel *everything*. I just hope you can for—"

Before he could finish, Paige jumped toward Carter and kissed him. His lips felt familiar and warm. As he held her face in his hands, she felt the weight of the past week lift off of her.

"Apology accepted," she said as she pulled back.

"You beat me to it," he replied as he leaned in for a second kiss.

"Well, I'll set out another mug for hot cocoa," Anne said from the hallway, catching the couple mid-make out.

Paige and Carter both blushed as they made their way inside.

After Carter had taken his things into Paige's room, he joined the rest of the family in the kitchen for some hot cocoa and a game of Phase 10.

"How do I look?" Carter said as he entered the room.

Paige was shocked when she turned to see Carter had added a Santa hat to his ensemble.

"Wow, so you really are getting into the Christmas spirit!"

"It's hard not to when the place I live in is drowning in Christmas decor," he replied with a wink. "I figured that on the chance my surprise visit worked and you let me in, I should be prepared with the proper attire."

"Well, you fit right in," Paige's mom said. "Now you just need to prove yourself with your gaming skills."

"Oh, you're on, Anne." Carter took a seat next to Paige's mom at the table, with Paige on his other side.

She reached next over and squeezed Carter's hand. He leaned over and whispered in her ear, "Merry Christmas," and gave her already blushing cheek a kiss.

***

The following week, Paige and Carter were back in Chicago getting ready for a New Year's Eve party at LondonHouse downtown. Carter had splurged on the tickets, insisting he wanted to take her out on a proper date. He had no clue at the time that this was the same location of her company Christmas party a year earlier where she learned about Chance's infidelity, but Paige was happy to replace the negative memory with a positive one.

For Paige, seeing Carter dressed up in a suit made it all worth it. She would have paid double the cost of the ticket for that sight alone.

Carter had stayed with Paige and her family for a few days following Christmas, soaking up the sun and the San Diego sights. They were like teenagers in love, walking the beaches, admiring the animals at the zoo, and stuffing their faces with tacos.

And on New Year's Eve, they drank and danced the night away, kissing every chance they could get.

Shortly before midnight, Carter led her to a quieter room. "There's something I've been wanting to talk to you about," he said. "You know I signed a lease for a new apartment a few weeks ago. Well, it turns out it's a tough lease to break, and also, I want to make sure that we give our relationship the best chance to succeed. So, I think it's best for me to move in there for now so we can each still have our own separate space for a bit and take things at the right pace."

Paige was slightly relieved to hear this. She had loved the days she'd spent with Carter in the condo and in California, but he was right—their relationship was in early stages, and moving too fast by continuing to live together could easily screw it up.

"As much as I'll miss waking up to your pancakes, I think you're right," she admitted.

"But before I go anywhere, I need to make sure of a couple of things first," he said. "For starters, according to our lease, I owe you a thirty-day *written* notice, so consider this my official notice." He got out his phone and sent her a text that said:

> This is my 30-day notice.

"Which means," he continued, "that you have another rent check coming your way. Hopefully it helps pad your freelance fund."

"Carter, you don't have to do that," she said.

"Oh, but I do. It's a contractual obligation after all." He gave her one of his signature smiles. "Plus, I want to. You're brilliant, Paige, and selfishly I don't want you seeing your ex-boyfriend five days out of the week."

"You and me both." She laughed and squeezed Carter into a tight hug.

"But most importantly," he said, pulling away from the embrace to look her in the eyes, "I don't want this move to be a step back in any way, so I officially want to ask if you would be my girlfriend."

aige smiled and said, "I thought you'd never ask."

They kissed as the countdown started, and Paige went into the new year as happy as she'd ever been.

Epilogue

Eleven months later...

"Just a little bit to the left. Perfect!" Paige said.

Carter and Linus stood up and looked at the new placement of the Christmas tree and gave each other a high five.

This year's Black Friday tradition looked different for Paige and Nadia, but in the best way. They had extended an invite to their significant others to join in the holiday cheer.

The boys even took part in the Christmas sweater tradition, each surprising the girls with the festive threads they found ahead of time.

"So, the countdown is on, guys," Carter said. "Just one month until the big day."

Being the Christmas lovers and romantics that they were, Nadia and Linus had settled on a Christmastime wedding. As maid of honor, Paige had a blast helping Nadia pick out all the festive decor.

"I know! It's crazy, right?" Nadia chimed in. "I can't believe it was just less than a year ago that we got engaged, and in the blink of an eye, I'll be walking down the aisle."

"And I'll be a blubbering mess at the other end of that aisle," Linus said, kissing his fiancée on the cheek.

"And we can't forget that today is Mr. Grinch's anniversary of trying to cancel Christmas." Nadia nudged Carter with her elbow.

"Yeah, I don't know if I'll ever live that down. Not my merriest moment, but I just needed someone to help me rediscover the Christmas spirit," Carter said as he slid his arms around Paige's waist and planted a kiss on the top of her head.

The last year had been one of Paige's favorites. Carter had moved out as planned in January, but still spent a substantial amount of time at Paige's condo. Their relationship had grown deeper in eleven months than her relationship with Chance had in three years. She and Carter had fallen deeply and madly in love, which was undoubtedly the highlight of her year.

But she had also quit her job in March to start her own freelance business, and it was off to a successful start. Paige had connected with a group of local female entrepreneurs, who ended up hiring her as a consultant for their own businesses. She was finally getting paychecks that reflected her experience and expertise. And Carter had been her biggest cheerleader along the way.

They spent another thirty minutes getting all the Christmas decorations up. Paige placed the last piece of garland on the mantel and sat next to Carter on the couch to admire the cozy decor.

The friends were planning on watching *Elf* that afternoon, so Nadia and Linus had gone out a few minutes earlier to grab a couple of bottles of wine and snacks. It wasn't lost on Paige that the last time she watched this movie on this couch, Carter felt far away on the other end. But today, she leaned into his warmth and couldn't believe how lucky she felt.

"Tell me, my love—anything special you want for Christmas this year?" Carter put his arm around her and pulled her close.

"This. I just want to be curled up right here with you." She closed her eyes and nuzzled her face into his chest.

"Well, it's funny you say that. I've been thinking . . . It's been nice to have our separate spaces this year while we really got to know each other, but I'm feeling ready to wake up with you every morning. I'm ready to hold you like this every night. If you're up for it, I'd love to be your roommate, again," Carter said as he held her even closer.

Paige beamed up at him. "Wait here," she said as she jumped up and ran into her bedroom. She returned several seconds later and handed Carter a small box wrapped up with a cute little bow.

"I was saving this for one of your Christmas presents, but after all this decorating today and what you just said, I don't want to wait." She could barely contain her excitement.

He carefully opened it to find a key inside, along with a note.

Will you be my roommate (again!) for Christmas?

Carter set the box down and kissed Paige as confirmation of his answer.

They had shared plenty of kisses over the last year, but this one felt like coming home.

Acknowledgements

Wow! My first book!

And what a fun book it is. As a long-time lover of cheesy Christmas movies I have enjoyed every single read through of this book. If you loved it even a sliver of as much as I did, then my mission is accomplished.

Now I want to take a moment to thank some people for making this book happen...

Karli Jackson, you are an editing wizard. You helped me take my crappy first draft and transform it into a *much* better and stronger book. Like, seriously. My first draft was a very below average book! You sprinkled your magic on it and guided me on becoming a better writer, and I'm so grateful for your partnership! Let's do another one soon, yeah?

Olivia, this book would quite literally not exist without you. Thank you for always entertaining and encouraging my random thoughts and always saying "yes" to Hallmark movies. In this case, you helped take my random thought and turn it into the plot of our very own cheesy

Christmas rom-com. I'm sure this is only the first of many plot lines we will come up with.

Veronica, you gave me the final push I needed to start my journey as an author, and it's been so, so fun getting to do this whole author thing at the same time as you. Plus, you were always a willing participant whenever I needed to do "research" by watching Christmas movies and rom-coms. Mega-bed hates to see us coming.

Liz, you were the exact early reader that I needed! The fact that you took the time to read through multiple drafts means the world to me. Thank you for all of your encouraging feedback—it gave me the confidence I needed to keep going.

To all of you who have cheered me on during this process and shown genuine excitement for this book, thank you. It's exactly what I needed to get this project over the finish line.

To my incredible Kickstarter supporters, thank you for believing in a first-time author.

For supporting the limited edition hardcover, I specifically want to thank: Will and Rachel Yeager, Gabe Van Dyke, Liz Van Dyke, Laura Sterenberg, Katie Slagle, Michelle Haynes, Caroline Malloy, Kylie Christianssen, Stephanie De Luna, Bridgett Briggs, Court Kuiper, Laura Jones, Amy Van Abbema, Rebecca O'Neill, Delaney George, Camilla Simon, Amanda Briggs, Olivia Ford, Jaclyn Lowry, Yigal Adato, Arianna Skentzos, Breighanna Minnema, Ann Lee Whitefield, and Kimberly Taylor.

And then a massive thank you to all of the Kickstarter supporters who named characters! I LOVED seeing what you came up with. Thank you Victoria Martin, Michelle Van Dyke, Nadia Geagea Pupa, Jennifer Van Tassel, Arvid Lundstrom, Logan Smith.

Last, but certainly not least, thank you to my family. To my parents, who have always supported and encouraged my creativity, and who are rarely without a book in hand. To my late grandmother, Carol, for passing on her passion for reading. And to my husband, Eduardo, for your constant support. Having you as my #1 fan makes me feel like the luckiest girl in the world.

About the Author

Aryn Van Dyke is an author and singer-songwriter obsessed with capturing love, heartbreak, and everything in between in words. Her albums I DO NOT NOT LOVE YOU and PULLING AT THE THREADS can be found on most streaming services, including Spotify and Apple Music.

When she isn't writing, Aryn teaches marketing strategy to authors and publishers around the globe with her company, Book Rockstar. She has lived in Nashville, Sweden, Amsterdam, London, and currently calls Grand Rapids, MI home. You can follow her music and writing updates on Instagram at @arynvandyke or by visiting www.arynvandyke.com.

More from Aryn

Get updates about *A Roommate for Christmas* and future books by Aryn by joining her email list.

Visit www.arynvandyke.com to become an email friend!

www.ingramcontent.com/pod-product-compliance
Lightning Source LLC
Chambersburg PA
CBHW022045240626
47154CB00007B/2576

* 9 7 9 8 9 9 1 3 1 9 6 3 8 *